DASHING FOR LOVE

Print ISBN: 979-8-9888570-5-1

Ebook AISN: B0DPRJ8W95

Cover Design & Illustration: Melissa Doughty - Mel D. Designs www. melissadoughty.com

Editor: Katie Awdas, Spice Me Up Editing

Published by Stafford Lane Publishing, LLC

For the Brat Pack.
The cowboy is your fault.

CHAPTER 1

GOLDIE

"**T**HE NAME IS Chad."

"You're...Chad?"

"Yeah, Chad. Nice to meet you." He slides onto the bar stool with an audible *oof*, taking longer to get situated than most before finally attempting a smile.

This isn't getting off to a great start. I mean, the dude's name is Chad. No offense to the Chads of the world, but I have yet to meet a good one.

Judging by the sweat on his upper lip, he's about to fall into the same no-good-Chad category.

But I'm a nice person. So nice, in fact, that I'm going to overlook the unfortunate sweat situation and focus instead on the fact that Chad's treating me to dinner at this really nice restaurant. And by *nice* I mean kind of mediocre with servers I could run laps around, but I'm trying really hard not to judge. I stick my hand out for a shake. "Nice to meet you."

His hand meets mine, and it's like shaking hands with a fish. Limp and damp.

I hold off the physical shiver of ick like the champion I am and beam at him. "How do you know Agatha?"

"Oh. Um, she's my mom's friend? From some kind of card night that all the old ladies play?"

I peer at him. "Are you asking me, or are you telling me?" I hate it when people make statements as though they're questions.

He squirms. "Telling?"

I look around for the server. I'm going to need a glass of wine to get through this. Or three.

One glass in and our buddy Chad hasn't gotten any better. He's not talkative, he answers all my questions with the least amount of words as possible, and I'm at my wit's end.

I've got to tell Agatha that she's not allowed to set me up on dates anymore. Now that it's me living in the tiny guest cottage behind her house instead of my sister Willa, she's decided that she needs to fix me up with the future love of my life the same way she set Willa up with Reid.

And honestly, I love her for thinking she set them up, but those two were on a collision course from the second they laid eyes on each other. Did Agatha lay the groundwork for more? Possibly. But to hear her tell it, she was who started the entire operation between those two.

With that victory under her belt, she immediately turned her sights to me. And I've endured my fair share of mediocre dates, but this one is by far the worst.

I focus back in on what Chad's saying.

"...so my bird, she's an African Grey and I've had her for twenty years—"

I hold up a hand. "Wait. You've had a bird for twenty years?" Maybe he *is* interesting.

He nods vigorously, his pale face lighting up a notch. "Yes! Her name is Affie because I had a lisp when I was little. I got her when I was twelve and she's been my best friend ever since."

Okay, I'm not gonna lie. That's kind of adorable. Is it making up for the rest of Chad's shortcomings? Not exactly. But it's hard to dismiss a guy who's managed a twenty-year relationship with a living creature.

"She sleeps in my room, and we talk every morning and night. She usually goes everywhere with me—she was pretty mad that I didn't bring her with me to our date. Said a lot of mean things about it, in fact." He chortles obliviously. "She doesn't even know you, but she does *not* like you."

I stop drinking wine. No amount is going to make this better, and why waste a perfectly good Uber charge when I can just stay sober and drive home?

Because dude just told me his parrot and him do everything together.

He keeps going. "And she loves the shower."

I blink. "Excuse me?"

He nods again, so hard his jowls shake. "Oh, she's a big fan of the shower. Just hops right in with me and when she's done, she hops out and waits on the towel rack."

I smile weakly. "Wow."

"Right? She's amazing. Just the other day, we were on one of our three daily walks around the property—that's what I call my backyard, ha, the 'property,' and..."

I zone out. After what feels like the entirety of the Paleozoic era, I pull out my phone and pretend I've gotten a call. "I'm so sorry," I frown and slip off the stool, grabbing my clutch and tucking it under my arm as I go. "I need to take this."

If he notices that I book it out of the restaurant like I've got a horde of wasps after me, he doesn't act on it.

Thirty minutes later, I'm back in my small town of Lucky and turning the Jeep's ignition off. I freaking *love* this thing. It's white with soft sides so that I can take advantage of the weather almost year-round, and of course it's got a line of rubber duckies going across the dashboard. I don't know who started that trend and I don't care; it's cute as all get out.

I let my hair down, sliding off the spare scrunchie I always keep in the Jeep and letting it fall to the console. Then I school my nerves and march up to Agatha's front door. The woman may be my landlord, but her fledgling career as a matchmaker needs to come to a stop. Immediately, if not sooner.

"Aren't you supposed to be on a date with Chad?" Agatha peers through the screen door.

"Hello to you, too, Agatha," I smile. "Are you going to invite me in, or shall we have our heart-to-heart on the porch?"

Her face falls. "Was it that bad?"

I sigh. "His name was *Chad*. What do you think?"

She steps onto the porch and toddles to the rocking chair. "Did he tell you about his African Grey?"

I take the other rocking chair and force myself not to screech at her like *I'm* a parrot. "You mean to tell me that you knew his name was Chad *and* you knew he had a parrot? Did you also know that they take showers together? And that she sleeps in the bedroom with him?" I lean closer and hiss. "It's no wonder he needs his mom to set him up on dates."

Agatha waves a dismissive hand. "I'm setting you up, too, missy."

I let out an aggrieved yelp. "Not because I *asked* you to!"

She sniffs. "You're not acting very grateful, Goldie. Your sister—"

"Has nothing to do with this," I interrupt, then take a deep breath. "Listen. I really appreciate your efforts on my behalf. Truly."

She purses her lips and assesses me. "Well. Okay."

"But I'd like you to stop. There's been Eric, the other Eric, and Steve, and Joe, and now Chad, and I"—I clasp my hands before me— "really need you to stop."

Letting out a deep sigh of her own, Agatha nods. "I suspected as much. I need to turn my talents elsewhere. They're clearly wasted on you."

It's a testament to my self-control that I don't jump up and let out an excited *whoop*. Truly. Instead, I bestow a gracious smile on the woman and slap my hands on my legs before standing. "Thank you, Agatha. I'm sure there's a young woman or two at church who'd just love your help."

Agatha's eyes go bright with anticipation. "Oh! You're right." She stands. "I need to call the girls. You have a good night."

She disappears through the door, dismissing me without another thought.

Well, that went easier than I thought it would.

I make my way around the house to the cottage I rent from Agatha, letting myself in and taking a shower, then pouring a much-needed glass of wine and cuddling up on the couch with a blanket and remote. Now that I'm home, I can relax.

Halfway through an episode of *Friends,* I get a text.

> **WILLA**
>
> Hey! You busy next Thursday? Matty's 30th birthday bash at Los Amigos. You need to be there.

> Count me in!

> Cool. Love you little sis

> Love you too big sis 

I toss my phone down and hit play on the episode again. I'd always had a crush on Joey—who didn't?—but my real crush growing up? Matty Brodigan. Always. I don't recall ever not liking him.

Now *there* was a man worth dating. He was always cute, and nowadays? Hubba hubba. Not to mention having a great personality, good job, and no African Grey in sight. Too bad Agatha doesn't want to set me up with him. But he's my sister's best friend, so that'll never happen.

CHAPTER 2

MATTY

WILLA

Lock up the clinic and get over here, birthday boy! We've got a pitcher of margaritas with your name on it!

I don't even like margaritas

Shots then. We have lots of shots. Get your ass over here old man

I don't like your tone

I do what Willa asks, checking to make sure everything is put away and the front is mopped clean of all the random slobber, fur, and occasional pee that makes its way in during the average vet clinic day. I'm pleasantly surprised to find that Liv, my receptionist, has taken care of it for me. She's supposed to do it every day, but sometimes it doesn't happen.

I walk into Los Amigos ten minutes later and find my best friends in the world: Willa Dash, her boyfriend Reid MacKinnon, and Goldie Dash, Willa's little sister. They all cheer as I make my way to them, making such a ruckus that the rest of the restaurant has no chance of missing what's going on.

"Happy birthday, old man!" Willa says gleefully, standing up to give me a hug.

"You're never going to get over me being a year older than you, are you?" I grin, squeezing her back.

She pulls away and laughs. "No way. Especially not now, when it matters."

Reid stands and claps me on the back. "Happy birthday, man. Welcome to my decade."

Goldie gives me a soft smile, staying seated and raising a margarita in my direction. "Happy birthday!"

I lean down to give her a kiss on the cheek, catching her perpetual scent of summer and sunshine in the process. "Thanks, Goldie." I take a seat next to her, then pour myself a margarita and tuck into the chips and dip.

Before long, the food is on the table and the evening is well underway, and I relax into the camaraderie. It seems I might just make it through the night without Willa doing something to embarrass me, which has been her usual approach over the last decade. But then, our server Carmen comes out with a cake and the restaurant's massive sombrero—brought out only for birthdays—and I know I'm sunk. The Mariachi band that comes every Thursday arrives at our table with a flourish, leading the entire restaurant in a rousing rendition of *Happy Birthday*. It's impossible to be mad, even if I don't love all the attention.

Beside me, Goldie angles out of her chair to light the candles while Willa aims her phone at me, capturing the entire thing. I wink at the camera, and then, holding the brim of the sombrero up, I blow them out and try like hell to ignore the twinge in my chest that wants something *more*.

A chorus of cheers and *Happy birthdays* ring across the restaurant as the candles go out. I should be happy. Grateful. I'm with my favorite people in the world, in the town I love, and I'm healthy. I shouldn't feel so…*greedy* for more. Maybe it's the milestone birthday that's got me so introspective. Maybe it's the fact that I still haven't gotten so much as a text from my parents acknowledging the day. I didn't expect one, not really, but there's no denying the sting of it.

Maybe some of it is that my best friend has Reid now. I'm incredibly happy for her, and she deserves everything in the world, but all that coziness is a little nauseating at times. Then there's Goldie. Willa and Goldie. Goldie and Willa. They've been my constants for years, and while Willa has truly only ever been a friend, there were a few quick times I've looked at Goldie and wondered. But I figure that's no good. Willa would have a conniption, for one thing. And Goldie? She's always been the life of the party, the exciting, interesting woman who can command an entire room the second she walks into it without even trying. She lives in technicolor, while I'm over here with a boringly steady life. It's only a matter of time before she's chasing news stories across the state, or even the country. There's no way a boring, steady guy like me even crosses her mind.

Not to mention all the romance novels that I can't stop inhaling. Liv left one at the office a few years ago, and I read the whole thing overnight. I was a zombie the next day, and when Liv figured out what happened, she started feeding me books. Damn things are addictive, and they're making me all googly-eyed.

I see Willa, and I read all these books, and all I can wonder is when my turn will come. If ever.

"Everyone, get together for a picture!" Carmen grabs Willa's phone and gestures for us to squeeze in. I'm between Goldie and Willa, like always, and Reid is on Willa's other side.

"This hat is ridiculous," Willa laughs, snuggling in and tugging Reid with her. "Get in, Goldie—we're sharing!"

Goldie scoots even closer, her cheek resting against mine as we all ham it up for the camera. As we all break apart, Goldie's soft smile captures my attention again.

"What's up?"

She meets my eyes. "Me? Nothing."

I look closely. Nothing's changed. "Are you sure? You're quiet."

She laughs as she scoots her chair back to her side of the table. "I'm *never* quiet, Matty. You're the quiet one, remember? Now slice up this cake!" She hands over the knife.

The flavor is carrot, my favorite, and it's a huge sheet cake, with plenty to dole out to everyone in the restaurant. We all know each other; it's impossible not to. I'm their vet.

"How's Sammie?" I ask Carmen about her schnauzer as I hand her a slice.

She beams. "He's great! Much better now that I've got him on that special food."

"Not feeding him leftovers from the restaurant is probably helping," I say with a grin.

After we demolish the cake, Carmen comes back with a round of tequila shots. Reid begs off, so I drink his. I only turn thirty once, right?

I might have another shot—things get a little fuzzy after a bit.

Is Goldie looking at me a little longer than usual?

Nah. That's wishful thinking.

Wait. Wishful? No. More like suicidal, because honestly, now that Willa's dating a cop, she could just ask for him to have me offed. The guy *was* undercover with a drug cartel, after all. He knows things. Techniques.

I snort. I'm *drunk*.

"Um, yeah, you are, big guy," Willa laughs.

I swivel my head to her. "Yup."

"I think that's our cue," Willa says, standing and waving for me to do the same. "Let's get you home."

"I'll drive," Reid says. "*All* of you."

Goldie makes a face. "I'm fine."

"I'm a cop, Goldie. Do you really think I'm going to let you drive buzzed?" Reid gives her a look that might make a lesser person shrink.

Goldie is definitely not that person. Giggling, she concedes. "You're right. Also, you're funny when you're growly."

He grins at her indulgently. "Okay, buzzed girl. Let's go."

Goldie and I climb into the back of Reid's F-150 and Willa takes the front. She turns to us as Reid pulls onto the road. "Goldie first, then you, yeah?"

I nod. At least, I think I do.

"Ooh, turn it up!" Goldie commands.

It's *Open Arms* by Journey. "Really?" Reid sighs.

Willa turns it up, and Goldie proceeds to belt the chorus at the top of her lungs.

All I can do is laugh, because Goldie may have a lot of amazing qualities, but being a good singer is not one of them.

She pokes me in the side and grins maniacally. "Join in!"

I shrug and join in, and I'm positive that Reid breaks the speed limit to get us home faster.

By the time I'm letting myself into my house, I've sobered up about five percent. Kitty, my German Shepherd, and Spot, my calico cat, greet me like they always do. My other cat, a grouchy orange tabby named Crush, stares at me in silent judgment from his perch on top of the couch as I walk past.

I give him a salute. He blinks and looks away.

I let Kitty out and feed and water all three, then check in on Hedgie, my hedgehog. He's ridiculously cute, and happily munches on the dinner I drop into his habitat.

A little later, I flop onto the couch and grab my laptop. My head is still pleasantly fuzzy, so it's the perfect time to create a profile on the app I've seen way too many advertisements for.

Blinding Love.

It's a stupid name, right? But the concept is that the app

won't let you see the person's face until you've talked for a certain length of time. And then, it only lets you post pictures that don't include your face. The whole thing's bizarre and no way can it actually work, but tonight? I need to be a little less boring.

In fact, that's my resolution for this decade: No more Boring Matty. No more all-work-and-no-play Matty.

Yeah. That sounds good. I can do this. I have no idea what being less boring looks like, but I can figure it out. Maybe I'll make a list.

My first step is this app. It can't hurt. Not like the women of this town are shoving each other down to go on a date with me, anyway. So I'll do it.

With a fake name.

Or at least, with a name that doesn't let the good people of Lucky know that their number one vet is using a blind date app. I may have resolved to be less boring, but there's no shaking off the pragmatism. We're not making miracles over here.

I pull it up and get to it.

Chapter 3

Goldie

W ILLA GLARES AT me when I skip into Dash In Diner the next morning for one of the few shifts I keep. Even though I'm full-time at the local paper, I can't quite give up waiting tables here; it's my family history, and I love it. Our parents started the diner before we were born, and even though Willa is in the process of buying it from them, they're still here, too. We've grown up here, the both of us gravitating into our respective areas: Willa in the kitchen with Dad, and me up front with Mom.

"Why are you looking at me like that?"

She points a chef's knife at me, bits of diced onions falling off the blade as she speaks. "Don't ever let me drink tequila and eat carrot cake at the same time."

I laugh. "Sounds like a you problem, Wills. I feel fine." And I do.

She huffs and goes back to chopping.

Mom sidles up and drops a container of silverware on the counter before me, and I grab a stack of napkins to start rolling.

"I hear that you told Agatha to stop setting you up," Mom starts.

I glance at Willa, who snorts and keeps her eyes on her work. "I did," I hedge.

"But I thought you were having such a nice time." Mom pouts as she speaks, throwing me a lower lip big enough to make a toddler proud.

I laugh. "Mom, I was having a *terrible* time."

She waves at Willa. "She complained about Reid, too, and look what happened!"

"Reid doesn't own an African Grey that he showers with," I shoot back.

Mom opens her mouth, then shuts it.

I shrug. "Exactly."

She sighs. "I just want both my girls happy. When I was your age—"

"Barbara," Dad calls from the back. "Leave her alone."

I giggle and beam in Dad's direction even though he can't see me. "Thanks, Daddy!"

Willa snorts again and Mom mutters to herself.

I give Mom a side hug. "Come on, Mom," I wheedle. "Don't be mad that your baby girl is single. It'll happen when it's supposed to."

Mom grumbles good-naturedly, then plants a kiss on my cheek. I know she means well, and in her defense, I was always the one with a steady string of boyfriends through high school, college, and a few years beyond that. But none of them ever stuck, and the past few years have seen most of the eligible guys get snapped up left and right. And honestly? It's okay. Mostly. For years, I was only ever out for a good time. I'm focused on the paper now, and that takes up a decent amount of time.

The clock makes its way to seven, and we open up. Tom and Jerry are first in, like they are every day, setting up at the end of the counter to gossip like two old hens and drink more coffee than can possibly be good for them. They're staples of Lucky, but even more, they're staples of the diner. If I didn't see the two of them posted up for hours at the diner on a daily basis, I think the world might actually stop turning.

Jerry pulls his ball cap off his nearly-bald head and sets it to the right of him on the counter. Tom adjusts his red suspenders before taking his seat next to his best friend and smiling broadly at me.

I pour their coffee. "What'll it be, boys?" They change their order every day, bless them.

"Jerry wants the hangover omelet," Tom says.

"And Tom wants the full breakfast, eggs over easy, toast extra crispy, bacon nearly black, extra butter in the grits."

I write their orders down with a grin, then put them in the wheel for Willa.

I hand Tom and Jerry over to Mom and handle the dining room. It's a relatively small diner, with a counter that seats eight, then ten four-tops and five two-tops in the dining room. When I'm waiting tables, I can usually handle it all without any issues.

Midway through the morning, my phone pings. I set down the orders for table seven, then pull my phone out as I walk back to the counter.

The notification is one that I haven't seen in, well, *ever*.

YOU'VE BEEN MATCHED

Huh.

It's the Blinding Love app. I stare at the words, in all caps and with no punctuation, and try to remember the last time I used the app.

Realization hits like a stack of pancakes, heavy and solid with a thud. *When I was with Annie.* Cousin Annie, who'd gone on to find someone who may not exactly be her happily ever after, but someone who is definitely making her happy a full year later.

I look at the words again.

YOU'VE BEEN MATCHED

It's the first time I've matched with anyone the entire time I've been on this app. And considering any time I turn other apps on, I match or get interest from people pretty much immediately, not matching with anyone on this one was pretty humbling at first. Am I so off-putting to people that my face is the only saving grace? But I got over it after a month of nothing happening—their loss—and eventually, I forgot all about the app.

I'm surprised the thing still alerted. *That's* how long it's been since I've used it.

Still. It's hard not to swipe open the app and see what the person I matched with is like.

The problem is that they'll see I've looked.

I shove my phone into my back pocket and keep working.

Ox shows up at lunchtime, bellying up to the bar like the massive man he is. Mom takes care of him, but I stop what I'm doing when I hear him mention his twin.

"Craziest thing," he's saying. "I'm surprised he even deigned to go on the show, let alone actually found love."

After glancing at the dining room to make sure all my tables are good, I turn my attention fully to Ox. "Start at the beginning," I demand. "Did you say Levi went on a show?"

Ox grins. "He did. There's this show that matches people up based on some application they fill out. Turns out that Levi matched with a woman he went to law school with—and he *hated* her back then," he chuckles.

I put my tray down and lean forward on the counter. "What happened?"

"Apparently, they had to stay in a pretty small house for twenty-four hours. Whole premise is to see if you want to try a relationship with the person after living with them for a whole day or not."

"And?" I urge, far more invested in this than I should be.

He smiles, and it's so genuinely happy that it makes my heart hurt. "They're together. Thin line between love and hate, and all that."

Jerry slaps the counter and leans into Tom. "Told ya!"

Tom scowls. "You didn't tell me squat, old man."

"I told you that Levi would find love before our Chief here."

"You said that twenty years ago after Levi got caught kissing your granddaughter behind the football stands," Tom grumbles. "That doesn't count."

Jerry sips his coffee contentedly. "Does, too."

I leave the old-timers to their bickering, my phone practically burning a hole in my back pocket. The timing of Ox's story feels almost like fate. If grumpy Levi Hall can find love in a twenty-four-hour television show, of all things, then what's stopping me from seeing who I matched with on Blinding Love?

Willa and I finish up at the same time, and I show her the notification as we're walking to our cars.

She doesn't hesitate. "Open it."

I bite my lip. I don't know why this feels different, but it does. "You think so?"

She shrugs, pulling her hair out of its ponytail and scratching her scalp with a satisfied groan. "You've already been set up on some doozies by Agatha."

"Not because I asked her to."

"No—you've just been too nice to tell her to stop."

"Until now," I point out.

"This can't possibly be any worse, right?"

I laugh sadly. "I want to be mad at you for saying that, but you're right. I'll do it."

Willa straightens and studies me. "Hey. This is probably gonna be great. You're Goldie. Beautiful, sunshine incarnate Goldie." She grins wickedly. "Whoever's on the other end won't know what hit 'em."

This time, my laugh is sincere. "You're right about that."

Agatha's waiting on me when I get home, calling out that she's got another nice boy for me if I'm interested.

And if *that* doesn't convince me to open the damn app, nothing will.

CHAPTER 4

MATTY

I T'S BEEN FORTY-eight hours since I created a profile on Blinding Love and about twenty-four since I matched with someone named Dawn. She seemed interesting, so I went for it. Problem was, the only thing the app would do is let me send a hello. Literally: Hello. I had one choice, and it was…Hello.

Cue the Lionel Ritchie soundtrack.

I'm not sure this thing is going to work. Especially since it's been a full day, and nothing has happened. I'm having serious regrets about the whole thing, and I'm *especially* having regrets about my decision to be less boring. I'm a small-town vet. Outside of emergency calls to farms or an unexpected litter of puppies getting dumped on the clinic's doorstep, how exciting can my life possibly get?

Bessie, the cow I'm inspecting at Farmer John's right now, doesn't seem to care one way or another that my match hasn't responded. She blinks her big brown eyes at me as I settle my stethoscope around my neck and look at the old man. "She's fine, John."

He peers at me, uncertain. "You sure?"

"Positive."

"Cause she was mooin' like she done been shot." He pulls his dirty red ball cap off and wrings it. "She's my best milker, Matty."

I thump her on the side and she blinks again. "Not a thing wrong with her."

"All right then. Might as well look at the rest of 'em while you're here." He turns and I follow, futilely attempting to avoid squishing my boots in the patties that Bessie and her compatriots have dropped.

My phone chirps and I pull it out, my eyes landing on the giant letters practically yelling at me on the screen.

YOUR MATCH RESPONDED

"Holy shit," I whisper, my heart doing a wild twisty thing as it leaps into my throat. Naturally, I trip over a rock, sending the phone flying out of my hand and landing perilously close to a pile of fresh poo. *That was close.*

"John, I'll be right over," I call, slowing my steps through the field to open the app.

John grunts and keeps moving.

DAWN

Hello

I stare at the simple word, wondering if that was all she was offered. Quirking a smile, I figure that's as good an intro as anything.

JAMES

Was "hello" the only choice you had, too?

She answers instantly.

Ha. Yes, it was. But it seems we've got the world
at our fingertips now.

Indeed we do. Thanks for responding.

Is this your first match?

Definitely. You?

I watch the dots on the app, indicating she's typing. I walk even slower, knowing that John will grow impatient but unable to tear my gaze away from my phone.

Tbh, I joined a year ago and never matched with anyone. I forgot about it. Had a whole existential crisis when the notification came through yesterday.

That explains the 24 hours you made me sweat.

Yeah I guess so.

"I got more to do than wait around on you, Matty!" John yells from the entrance into the horse barn.

"Coming!"

I'd like to keep chatting, but I'm at work. Can I text you later?

You work on Saturdays?

I wince. I don't want to give too much away at first.

Sometimes.

After a minute, she answers.

Sure, text me later. Have fun at work!

Thanks.

Then, before I can spiral too much, I add a smiley emoji at the end of it.

I spend the next hour looking over the horses and giving them their scheduled vaccinations, John close by and watching me like a hawk, which is standard. The man is nothing if not thorough.

"You remember that little slip of a dog I told you about last month?"

"The chihuahua you found?" I clarify.

He nods and runs a hand over his gray beard. "I don't think it's going to work out here."

"Why not?" Finished with the last horse, I begin packing up all my supplies.

"Thing's gonna get trampled or ate, and I don't know which one. Plus, it keeps shakin' like it's scared half to death. Hell, maybe he is."

"Where is he?"

"Kept it in the house today. Figured that was best."

I sigh and gesture for him to lead the way. "Well, let's see him."

The second John opens the small house's door, we're greeted by the little cream-colored dog. He's yapping happily, bouncing and vibrating. John scowls at him. "There he is."

I grin and scoop him up. He's a tiny thing, maybe three pounds if I'm being generous. "Hey there, killer."

The apple-headed dog yips and licks my face, his bulbous black eyes bright and intelligent.

I laugh. He's the most ridiculous-looking little thing I've seen in quite some time, and I've seen my fair share of adorable pets.

"Seems he likes you," John says.

"Seems so." I know where this is going, and I'm okay with it. Finding this little guy a home won't be hard. "Want me to take him off your hands?"

John's answering smile tells me plenty. "I'll get you his food." When he returns with the food, he's also kitted out a cardboard box with a blanket that he holds out to me. "Figure he can ride in this."

Narrowing my eyes, I ask, "Just how long have you been waiting to foist this dog off on me?"

John looks askance. "Dr. Brodigan. You know I am an animal lover."

I wave him off with a laugh. "I'm kidding, John. I know you are. Help me get him to the truck?"

Soon enough, I'm securing the box to the front seat of my truck and driving off John's property, the tiny cream chihuahua staring at me adoringly as we go.

I shake my head. I'm the world's biggest sucker.

LATER, AFTER I'VE INTRODUCED THE CHIHUAHUA TO the other animals in the house—Kitty is excited, though the little dog is more than a little terrified of Kitty, Spot is indifferent, and Crush is murderous, all to be expected—and showered, I pull the Blinding Love app back up.

JAMES

Hey, look at that—still get to use more than Hello

After a few minutes, the notification chimes and I grin, falling onto the couch with the chihuahua tucked into my chest.

James! You're back.

I grimace. Yeah, James is what I went with. It's my middle name, and I figure that's not *too* deceptive, right? I can't use my real name yet.

JAMES

All done with work and relaxing at my house.

Glad to hear it. I'm hard at work relaxing in my
house as well.

Now is when we're supposed to engage in witty
banter, right?

Ha, something like that. You got any?

Hang on. I'm checking my pockets.

Nope, no banter in my pockets. Found a dollar,
though, so I guess that's something.

Nice. That'll get you a sample bite of fudge at the
Fudge Shoppe in Lucky.

You know Lucky?

I do…

Does that ellipsis mean you don't want to tell me
more?

It does. Can't give too much away just yet, right?

I can't stop the grin that spreads on my face.

Couldn't agree more.

Look at you — a man who knows how to pick up
on a woman's subtle hints.

I laugh and scratch the chihuahua's knobby little head, chuckling at the happy snuffle he makes. I'm already a goner. No way am I going to place him with anyone else. He's way too cute, and he's the chillest chihuahua I've ever met. Now I just have to come up with his name. I turn back to the conversation with Dawn.

> Not to brag, but I'm known for my ability to pick up subtle hints.

> You're funny 😐

> Can I screenshot that? My friends will never believe it otherwise.

> Lol sure, go for it.

My stomach rumbles, ready for dinner, but I can't make myself get up just yet. I'm enjoying the conversation too much. I spend the next hour talking to Dawn, and by the time we finally sign off, I'm amazed. I've never been able to talk to anyone so easily.

Well, no one other than Willa. And Goldie, too, I suppose. But those are the only two women—hell, *people*—I've ever been that comfortable with. I mean, I'm a vet because I like animals better than most humans. They never let you down. Humans? They're a whole other story.

I shrug off the momentary blip of sadness and focus on the good things in life. Things I got by relying on myself and myself alone.

CHAPTER 5

GOLDIE

Sundays are yoga and a pier walk day. It used to be a sacred thing that Willa did only with Matty, but once Reid came into the picture, all bets were off. And I need the mental and physical release of yoga, especially after I spent hours yesterday hunched over my phone like a love-struck teenager.

James is fun. He's easy to talk to and seems genuine. Could I be getting catfished? Of course. But it seems like it'd be a lot of trouble to go to on this app. For now, I'll take it nice and slow.

Regardless, I could use the stretching of mind, body, and spirit, so off to yoga I go. Willa and Reid are already there, with their black cat Midnight picking her way through the mats like she owns the place. Reid brought her in here when he was co-parenting her with Willa, and the owner basically couldn't say no to Reid's muscles, so there you have it.

The whole town had the hots for Reid back then, and it's easy to see why: He's cute as hell, has dimples that might be as deep as the ocean, he's fit, and looks damn good in running shorts. A couple of people—Willa and my mom included—were all for *me* and Reid getting together when he first got here, but it became obvious very quickly that he was down bad for my sister. And thank goodness, because she was just as bowled over by him.

I give Willa a hug hello, and she immediately asks, "Did you talk any more with James?" Her eyebrows wiggle.

I laugh. "A little, yeah. He sent me a good morning message this morning, and I sent him one back." I unroll my mat. "It's good. Nice and slow."

Willa hums and we get situated. Reid joins us, taking the other side of Willa, and I glance at the space beside me.

"Where's Matty?"

Willa shrugs and Reid says, "He'll be here. Guy wouldn't miss it."

A commotion starts up at the front, followed by squeals and a tiny yip. Seconds later, Matty appears, a grin on his face.

My heart does the same squeeze thing it always does when I see him. I've resigned myself to it. It's normal to have a crush on your sister's best friend, right? It might not be normal that I've had it for over twenty years, but whatever. The heart wants what it wants, I guess. Unfortunately, my heart refuses to listen to me when I tell it over and over that Matty Brodigan is off-limits. Always has. Always will.

It doesn't stop me from appreciating the man. Like every time he's at yoga, today he's wearing running shorts over spandex shorts and a fitted workout shirt. He's in shape but not bulky, and he's tall but not overly so, probably an even six feet if I had to guess. I'm a solid five-five, and I've stood next to him enough to know that if I were ever lucky enough to kiss the guy, we'd fit together perfectly. I might have to go on my tiptoes, and he might have to bend a bit, but hey, what's a little compromise, right?

Not that I'll ever get to kiss him. Some other woman will do that. She'll run her hands through his wavy mess of brown hair, and she'll probably think he needs to trim it. (He doesn't.) And she'll get to stare into his gorgeous brown eyes, the ones that look like whiskey on ice in the daylight and dark caramel at night. She might tease him about almost always wearing cowboy boots and jeans, instead of appreciating the way his ass and thighs fill the denim out.

I hate her. I don't know who she is, but I hate her all the same.

A tiny tapping of nails on the hardwood floor has me snapping out of my hatred for a future woman, and I focus on the sound. Running around like an adorable vision of utter and complete cuteness, is a tiny cream-colored chihuahua. Strutting about like he owns the place.

Matty laughs as he comes to unroll his mat next to mine.

"Is that yours?" I ask, unable to contain the glee in my voice.

"Yep," he answers. "His name is Killer."

I whack him on the arm. "Stop it. You can't be that cute."

He rubs his arm and his eyes freaking *twinkle*. "You think I'm cute, Goldie?"

I roll my eyes and turn away, hoping he doesn't see the blush that blooms at his teasing.

Yoga isn't nearly as calm as it normally is, with Killer getting the zoomies and chasing Midnight through the mats. There are more than a few yelps and hisses, but lots of laughing at the duo's shenanigans all the same. As we leave, Matty promises the owner he'll leave Killer at home next time. He produces a leash for the walk on the pier, and I take a deep breath to center myself.

Focus on James. Not your sister's best friend. The guy I *can* have versus the guy I can't.

Willa threads her arms through Matty's and leans her head on his, saying something too quiet for me to catch. They laugh, then Reid gathers her to his side, likely smushing Midnight as she's riding in the carrier strapped to Reid.

I shake my head. These two men are something else: a big cop wearing a cat and a tall, hot vet walking a tiny dog.

Matty slows and looks back for me, and I throw on a smile. "Coming!"

It's a beautiful early spring day, just warm enough in the sun to not need long sleeves, and I tip my head up to soak in the rays. Seagulls call to each other as waves lap against the pylons. It's quiet when it's not tourist season, and aside from the guy fishing off the end of the pier, we're the only ones here.

This is one of my favorite times of the week. We walk, catch up on each other's lives, and make up stories about the people who own the yachts docked down one side. I revel in it, and in the closeness we all have. Reid's appearance in Lucky changed so many things for all of us, and I couldn't be more grateful. Thanks to him, Willa came out of her shell and managed to talk Mom and Dad into setting plans for retirement. They refuse to completely stop working, but the diner is slowly transitioning to Willa, and she's thriving. Seeing her take control of her life was what inspired me to ask JJ for a job at the paper, even though the paper was little more than a gossip rag at the time.

"How's it feel being thirty, old man?" Willa asks Matty.

Beside her, Reid growls playfully. "Watch it. I'm still the oldest one here."

Willa grins at Reid and turns her attention back to Matty.

"Same as it felt being twenty-nine," Matty answers. "How's it feel being mean to your best friend?"

"I just wanna know if you need a dog sitter," I say, reaching down to pick Killer up. "Because if you do, I'm in."

Matty's whiskey eyes meet mine. "He's kind of irresistible, isn't he?"

You have no idea.

After two circuits of the pier, Willa and Reid take off. Killer strains at the leash, clearly wanting to go around again, and I laugh as Matty contemplates him. "I'll keep you company if you want."

He doesn't hesitate. "That'd be nice."

I tamp down the flare of excitement that always rises at the chance of being alone with Matty. *Remember James. James, James, James.*

I clear my throat. "Great!"

We start walking, and Matty asks, "How's the job going?"

"Good. Finally starting to write articles that have a bit more heft to them than the regular gossip JJ's so fond of, and that's nice."

"I'm sure anything you do is an improvement over whatever JJ's got going on," he says, smiling over at me. "You'll be jet-setting all over the state and country before long, doing heavy-hitting pieces that change hearts and minds."

The compliment warms my entire body, but I make myself wave it away. "I'm just glad to finally put my degree to use."

"What kept you from it?"

I blink up at him. "I'm not sure anyone's ever asked me that."

"No one?"

"Well, I take that back. Willa did."

After a beat, he prompts, "You gonna answer me?"

I shrug. "It's hard to explain, but I guess the easiest way to put it is I didn't feel like I was ready. I felt...young, you know? Maybe it was running after you and Willa all those years," I joke.

"You're only two years younger."

"Right," I hedge. "But still. Lucky is such a small town, and four years at college in the same state only goes so far to help a girl with personal growth. And I know what people think of me."

Matty stops, and the expression on his face is very much Concerned Older Brother.

I hate it.

"What do you mean, you know what people think of you?"

I can't look at him. "Same way they always have. I'm the blond, the airhead, the opposite of Willa. You know."

He frowns. "No. I don't know."

I release a frustrated sigh. "Forget it."

"Goldie—"

I shake my head. "Seriously, drop it. I don't even know why I'm all up in my head about it. It's fine." I force a smile and a laugh. "I promise."

He doesn't look convinced. "No. You are perfect. You are unafraid to be *you*. And that's...that's worth being proud of. Anyone who has ever made you feel like you're anything other than phenomenal is an asshole."

I suck in a breath. *What?*

He blinks, seeming almost startled at his own words. With a jerk of his chin, he turns and starts walking again.

I close my mouth and fight back the unexpected wave of emotion that threatens to overtake me.

He turns back to where I'm rooted to the spot. "Goldie—"

"I should go." I step back from him, needing to breathe air that isn't Matty Brodigan. "Sorry."

"Don't apologize." His voice is soft as he gestures at me. "If anything, I should apologize for making you uncomfortable."

I bark out a laugh. "Of course you'd say that. God, you're unbelievable."

He furrows his brow. "Me?"

I take another step away. *Unbelievably perfect.* "I'll see you around, Matty."

He opens his mouth, but I turn away. I can't begin to explain what just happened, only that it needs to stop.

Chapter 6

Blinding Love

MATTY

What do you call a cow with no legs?

GOLDIE

That's a heck of a way to say good morning 😌

Come on, Dawn—answer the riddle.

Ground beef 🐮

Ha! So you, too, know the joy of a really bad joke.

Indeed

I have another question…

Is it a riddle? Because if that's what we're doing, then watch out—I've got some doozies.

It's not, but noted.

Okay, what's the question?

Do you have the option to add a photo to our
chat now?

Hang on

Oh, wow—yeah. That's new.

I guess maybe this is the app's way of rewarding
us for talking to each other for a week.

Maybe so. Doesn't that go against the whole
"blind" part of this app's name?

We're not supposed to upload photos of
ourselves.

What, did you look at the rules or something?

...

omg you *did*

James, you're a—gasp!—rule follower!

Okay, okay, be nice

I think it's sweet. Very…rule-followy of you.

Are we making up words now?

Why not? We're grown-ups. We can do what we
want.

Bring on the chaos!

Exactly

But…back to the option to add a photo

Okay, what are you thinking?

A photo of our faces is out.

Okay. Any other body parts? Is now where the app starts to be like those other apps • •

Whoa now. What are you sending on those other apps? Wait—are you on other apps??

Lol no, I'm not on any other apps. But you know how guys are.

Pretend I don't.

Okay, you're playing the innocent right now, I see how you are

Seriously, Dawn, explain it to me like I'm five.

Dick pics, James. Are you saying you want to send me a dick pic?

Jesus! No!

I think I'm traumatized

You're traumatized? Try being on the receiving end of those things. I get them in random Instagram messages.

Holy shit. Seriously?

What, you thought it was an urban legend or something?

No…I don't know what I thought.

Welcome to the internet, James. It's a wild place out here.

Clearly.

What I'm getting out of all this is that you won't be sending me a dick pic.

That's *exactly* correct

Then what would you propose we send?

How about something related to our jobs?

We've not told each other what we do, though—
are we ready to do that?

How about we let the photos speak for
themselves?

Gold star for vagueness, James

Fair. I'm still freaking out over here

Why?

I don't know.

Okay, *now* you get a gold star because you're a
man who just admitted he doesn't know
something.

Me admitting I don't have a good reason for
something isn't worthy of a gold star. If anything,
I probably deserve a whack upside the head.

Hmm. You might be right.

I know what picture I'll send, though—I guess
I've got that going for me?

Sure. But I want to go first.

Okay, send when you're ready.

[photo of a close-up of the base of the clock
tower in Lucky's town square]

Um, what is that?

If I told you, it'd be a pretty big hint for exactly where I live.

Interesting. Hold on while I obsess over it.

Ha. Your turn.

[photo of a brown horse looking at the camera]

omg that's a horse!

Lol very good.

Aw, it's beautiful. Boy or girl?

Girl

Clearly you're a cowboy

Wait

Nope—that's it. Cowboy. A cowboy who lives in Southern Alabama. Because that's super practical.

Hey, it's possible

So you *are* a cowboy?

Not exactly

Okay, you're not exactly a cowboy, but you're not *not* exactly a cowboy?

Um…maybe? I'm not sure what I'm admitting

You've just confirmed you're a cowboy. Do you have cowboy boots?

Yes

Are you wearing them right now?

Lol yes, in fact I am

Ha! See? You're a cowboy. You sent me a picture
of a horse and you're a cowboy

Again: not exactly

Agree to disagree

Want me to tell you the horse's name?

Sure

Peppermint

Well, that's adorable

She's a good horse.

Where is she located?

Oh, I see what you're doing there—nice try.

It was worth a shot.

Though technically, I could tell you where
Peppermint is, and you'd still not know where I
live.

Wait—how do I know that the photo is even
yours? Like, you could have just grabbed that off
the internet.

That's true. I didn't, but how can I prove it?

You need something to show today's date. Then
put that in the photo with Peppermint.

What, like a newspaper? When are we?

Ha ha. Newspapers are still a thing, you know.

They are, but I can't put my hands on one right now. I'm in a barn. Pick something you'd find in a barn and tell me what that is, then I'll send a picture of it

Okay, but what if I don't know what's typically found in a barn?

A barn with horses. Does that help?

Hay?

Okay, hang on.

[photo of hay in front of Peppermint's face]

I gotta tell you, James, you are not the best photographer

That's fair

But I believe you now. You're a real cowboy.

That backfired spectacularly

Lol it's going to take a lot to convince me you're not one.

I sent you two photos—send me another?

Nah

Nah?! Rude.

Hey, you offered that second photo.

Only to prove that I wasn't catfishing you.

All the same…

Fair enough. I do need to get back to what I'm doing.

Is it your job? Are horses your job?

...

HORSES ARE YOUR JOB?!?!

Maybe, maybe not.

Ughhhh James you're killing me

Just keeping the mystery alive, Dawn

Something like that. But yeah, we should
probably act like we have jobs to do.

Can I text you later tonight?

Sure. Give Peppermint a kiss for me.

Will do.

CHAPTER 7

MATTY

ON MONDAY, I go to the Dash In Diner for lunch. Not a week goes by that I'm not here at least once, but if I'm being honest, it's more like three or four times.

What can I say? When the cook is your best friend, *and* she's talented as hell, you belly up to the counter a little more than might be good for you.

Besides, if I come during the work week, I always bring Liv something back. That counts...for something.

As always, Tom and Jerry are still there. Those guys are here every day, nearly open to close, without fail. They're as much a part of the diner as Willa, Barbara, Dean, and Goldie. Although now that Goldie's got her job at the paper, I see her less than before. I can't stop myself from looking for her, though.

Reid and Ox are also at the counter, and as fate would have it, there's an empty stool between the two sets of men.

"Happy Monday, guys."

"Is it, though?" Ox groans.

Reid chuckles. "He's just mad because this whole Chief thing is a lot harder than Uncle Jack made it out to be."

Jerry snorts. "Chief Mac never said it was a cakewalk."

"Just made it look that way," Tom finishes with a smirk.

Ox leans over to glare at them. "You two are the rabble rousers that are causing me all the trouble, so I'd appreciate it if you simmered down."

I smile gratefully at Barbara as she pours me a cup of coffee, then tip the cup at Ox. "Do tell us of all your troubles, Great Chief Hall."

Reid laughs, and Ox grumbles. "They want a new clock tower."

"Damn thing ain't kept proper time since the fifties!" Jerry exclaims.

"You'd know, you old geezer," Ox shoots back.

"I'm gonna get Goldie on this—it's a scoop," Tom declares.

"None of this is your lane, *Chief*," I remind him.

He raises a thick eyebrow. "You clearly haven't been attending the town halls, or you'd know that these two"—he flicks a dismissive hand at the old men to my right— "have made it my lane."

"Okay, let's change topics," Reid says, patting Ox on the shoulder. "Before Chief Hall comes up with a reason to arrest you two. I need a handyman. Who do you recommend?"

"Probably Jim down at the hardware shop," Ox says.

"His daughter's better than he is." Heads swivel to me. "What? It's true. Darcy is an actual carpenter. She knows her way around a house. Assuming that's the kind of handyman you're after."

"Ooh, Darcy," Ox muses, then grins. "She and my brother hate each other."

"Which one?" Reid asks.

"Anthony."

"Why?"

Ox shrugs. "Have you met my brother? Bigger than me, grumpy as hell, grunts more than he speaks?"

Reid chuckles. "Fair."

"Didn't they date?" I venture.

"Speaking of dating." Tom waggles his eyebrows.

Barbara slides the patty melt and fries I didn't have to order in front of me. I look up and smile a *thanks* at Willa. She tips her head in response. Then I look back at Tom. "What are you babbling about now?"

"When are you gonna settle down?" Jerry asks. "Have some babies?"

"See?" Tom says proudly. "We don't just ask the women."

"No, you're equal-opportunity inconsiderate asses," I joke.

Reid quirks a grin. "Ignore them."

"Easy for you to say—you're locked in."

His smile broadens and softens at the same time as he steals a glance at Willa. "Yeah."

I chuckle and take a bite of my sandwich. "You're so gone for her it's not even funny."

"Without a doubt," Reid agrees. "And it's the fucking best. Just you wait." He levels a meaningful look at me, and I shove fries in my mouth so I don't have to think about what that look could possibly mean.

My phone dings when I'm finishing lunch, and while I hate to do it, I *am* on break, so I pull it out of my pocket to see if it's Liv at the clinic.

It's not. It's an alert from the Blinding Love app, telling me I've got a photo to look at.

The way my heart rate speeds up should concern me. But I really like this girl. We chat so easily every day, and even though we've kept who we are pretty much hidden from each other, we've started to wade into deeper territory. And I have to hand it to the app—we really do have a lot in common.

The guys are all distracted talking to each other, so I open the app to see the photo. It's a shiny copper penny, heads-up on a street.

DAWN

Today's good luck charm

I smile and start to write back, when Reid leans over. "What's that?"

I blacken the screen. "Nothing."

"Oh, that's way more than *nothing*. Ox, I think our boy might be chatting it up with someone."

Ox perks up. "Ooh, who are we talking to?"

I try to will away the heat creeping up my neck and repeat, "It's nothing. I'm not talking to anyone."

Reid and Ox look at each other, then stand. Before I can process what they're doing, they've each hooked my arm in theirs and are walking me out of the diner.

Tom and Jerry hoot behind me. "Get him, boys!"

I barely have to walk for as tight a grip the guys have on me. "Remind me never to actually get in trouble with you two."

Reid opens the door. As we go outside, I ask, "Is this legal?"

Ox laughs. "We're not arresting you."

"But we *are* getting the story out of you."

They let me go and I straighten myself, then point at Reid. "You were never this nosy when you first got here."

Reid smirks. "Consider it payback for your meddling, then."

"Fine," I sigh, running a hand over my face. "But you two need to keep this between us. No one else. Not even Willa."

"Wow, keeping something from your best friend?" Ox says. "This I gotta hear."

"I joined a dating app."

They both look at me, waiting. "And?" Reid prompts.

Oh. Maybe this isn't the big deal I'm making it out to be. "It's called Blinding Love. They match you based on a big profile you fill out, and you don't get to see pictures of the person until you're a certain number of messages and time in."

"I've heard of that," Ox says. "Honestly thought of using it myself. It's not easy trying to find someone."

"Exactly."

"But I thought I saw a picture," Reid notes.

"You did. The app won't allow photos of faces yet, but we can post pictures of other things. I've been talking to someone for a week."

"What's their name?" Ox asks.

"Dawn."

Ox looks at Reid. "You hear how he said it?"

Reid smirks at me. "You like her."

I groan. "Are you two twelve? Yes, I like her. It's only been a week, but so far, yeah. She's...she's pretty great."

"What are the odds that I have two people in my world who are doing dating things?" Ox muses. "First, my brother in that wild twenty-four-hour business, and now you in the Blinding Love app. I think I'll do it."

I start. "Seriously?"

"Why not? I have nothing to lose. And you seem pretty happy."

"This isn't a big deal, Matty. It's a dating app. Why don't you want to tell Willa again?" Reid asks.

I shrug. "I don't know. I just...don't. I'm invoking bro code. You two have to keep it to yourselves—even if you sign up, Ox."

"Bro code? *Now* who's the twelve-year-old?"

Ox shrugs. "Doesn't bother me any, but for the record, I think it's weird you're being secretive about it."

"Fine," Reid agrees. "It's nice to see you getting out there. Though, I gotta admit, I thought you and Goldie had a thing when I first got here."

I nearly choke. "Goldie? And me?" He's far too close to the desire I'll never let myself fully explore. Because something about it feels...not *wrong*, exactly, but...forbidden? She's beautiful—stunning, if we're being honest. Long, sun-kissed blond hair and a smile that is tailor-made to get her whatever she wants. She makes me feel like a troll in comparison. But we grew up together, and she's my best friend's little sister. And again: far too adventurous and fun to be interested in a boring guy like me.

"Yep. Something about you two. But maybe I was seeing things."

"Nah. There's something," Ox states.

"What? No there isn't."

Reid puts his hands up. "Whatever you say, Matty."

I shake my head. "You two are buying my lunch after all this. I gotta get back to work."

Laughing, Reid and Ox head back inside. I hop in my truck and start the engine, but don't leave until I respond to Dawn.

CHAPTER 8

GOLDIE

IN A SHOCKING turn of events, I somehow convince my sister to join me at Hall's Balls on Friday for drinks and greasy food that she didn't cook. We arrive together, having shared an Uber from my cottage.

"I always forget about this place," Willa says as we walk in, looking around.

"Seriously? It's the best of all the worlds. Classic arcade and pinball games over there, a dozen pool tables over there, and a full bar to go with it. How could you not love it?"

She raises a shoulder. "Since when have I been the type of person to spend her time somewhere like this?"

I snort. "Fair. Come on—the bar awaits."

Ox's oldest brother, Anthony, is the owner and bartender, and I force a bright smile his way as we sit down. He's massive: bigger than his younger brothers and has much more of a gruff exterior. Where Ox is all goofy muscle and his twin is polished muscle, Anthony is more like…terrifying muscle. Despite my ability to charm just about anyone, Anthony has never been one of those, and he's a little intimidating.

The fact that he rarely smiles most definitely has something to do with it.

"Drinks."

I keep my own smile in place to answer what I presume was his version of a question. "Hi, Anthony!"

He grunts.

"What are we drinking, sis?" Willa asks.

"Let's get…the Pink Thing," I decide, figuring if it's on the board behind Anthony, he won't be mad about making it.

He grunts again and turns, plucking the bottle of vodka off the shelf behind him as he goes.

"What's in it?" Willa whispers.

"Don't know," I whisper back. "I was trying to pick something that would keep Anthony from growling at me, but I don't think it worked."

The drinks are in front of us within moments, the martini glasses chilled and filled to the brims with a frothy pink concoction. "Enjoy," Anthony demands, then moves down the bar.

We raise our glasses. "To blind date apps," Willa says with a smile.

I grin. "Cheers." I take a sip, and it's delicious. Delicate and fruity, with absolutely no hint of the alcohol in it.

"Whoa. That's dangerously good," Willa declares. After another sip, she sets the glass down and spears me with one of her signature *I'm older than you* looks. "So. How are things going with James?"

"Good. He's so easy to talk to and funny. Super considerate. I swear, half the time I think he's gotta be a woman—he's far too emotionally mature to be a guy," I laugh.

"You're not using your real name, right? What if his name isn't even James?"

I shrug. "I assume it's not. There's a level of trust I've gotta have, you know?"

"I get it, but why don't you two just come out and tell each other who you are already? What's the hold-up?"

I consider the question. "It's hard to say. I think both of us are comfortable with the pace."

Willa snorts. "A snail moves faster. Seriously. Hasn't it been two weeks? And you still don't know what he does?"

He's a cowboy, I think with a grin.

Willa points at me. "What's that expression for?"

"Just thinking of something we've talked about. He does something with horses, but that's about all I've gotten out of him."

"Horses?"

I nod and take another sip. "Horses."

She narrows her eyes at me. "There's more to it than that, but I'll leave it alone for now. I have to pee." She slides off the stool and heads in the direction of the bathroom.

I consider her words. Yes, James and I are moving slow, but it's actually really nice. I like being forced to get to know him. Sure, we could have traded phone numbers and gotten off the app way before now, but I *like* that we've both followed the rules and allowed the app to set the pace.

Willa returns, waving a flyer. "Look."

I inspect it. "Ooh, a masquerade ball? Fun!"

"Raising money for the food bank," Willa confirms. "Next week. You should invite your mystery man."

I consider it. "That's…not a bad idea, actually."

Willa smiles. "Thanks. Do it now."

"Now?"

"Yeah," she urges. "Why not?"

I grin. "You know, I like this version of you."

"Which version is that?"

"The one where you're all pushy and confident and stuff."

Her cheeks tinge pink. "Aw, thanks."

I pull out my phone and snap a picture of the flyer, then send it to James through the app.

DAWN

Wanna go?

JAMES

That's a big step forward

I think we're ready for it

Do we keep masks on the whole time? Keep the mystery going?

I bite my lip and tilt the screen to Willa.

She scrunches her face. "I think you need to show each other who you are. This is kind of nuts."

"But I enjoy the mystery," I protest. Holding the phone back up, I point to James's text as proof. "So does he."

Willa takes another sip and eyes me. "It's up to you. If he kidnaps you, then I'll get to say I told you so."

I chuckle. "Yes, of course. I'll be sure to let you know if he kidnaps me." I type my answer back.

Let's do it. Keep the masks on. No giving ourselves away just yet.

Okay, I'm in.

Perfect. Is it weird that I'm excited about this?

Is it weird that I'm excited you're excited?

Talk to you later 😊

Talk to you later 🤠

I snort and let Willa see the exchange.

"What's the deal with the cowboy smiley face?"

Snickering, I lock the screen and tuck it into my purse. "Inside joke."

She raises an eyebrow. "You've got inside jokes, too?"

My belly warms. "Yeah," I confirm. "We do."

"Drinks." Anthony is back and glaring at us.

Willa considers. "I can do one more if I text Reid to come get us. You?"

"Let's do it."

CHAPTER 9

MATTY

I'M OUT AT an alpaca farm when I get an alert that Dawn's sent a photo. It takes everything I have not to shove the animal away from me and yank out my phone to see what she's sent. I'm worse than Pavlov's dog when I hear the alert. But I keep myself together, and when I finish the check-up of a particularly feisty male alpaca—did you know those guys can spit five feet? It's gross—I pull it up.

It's a picture of a lacy black masquerade mask, and the things it does to my insides should concern me.

Suddenly, one of the alpacas behind me sneezes, and I flinch.

TJ, the farmer, starts laughing. "I think he got you, Doc."

I reach up and feel the mucus on the back of my ball cap. And because I'm a professional, I squirm and make an *ew* sound. TJ laughs even more as I pull my hat off and cuss. It's covered in alpaca snot.

Folks, there are precious few things that can ruin a ball cap. Alpaca snot is one of them. I cuss and look at the cap in disgust.

TJ waves me to come with him. "Come on. I've got a spare hat you can borrow."

I follow him to the barn, tossing the ball cap in the trash bin as we go, and he produces a well-worn cowboy hat from a clutter-filled work area. I throw it on with a thanks. "How do I look?"

The old man chuckles. "Like a vet playing at being a cowboy."

"Perfect," I laugh. "Let's finish these check-ups."

It's another hour of checking on the animals, because TJ and his wife Sue run the state's only major alpaca farm and it's quite the operation. By the time we're done, I'm a grimy mess, but that's pretty standard for farm days. I wouldn't trade it for anything. I love the animals I get to see at the clinic, but it's a whole different ballgame when you're staring down a herd of alpacas, chasing goats, helping a cow give birth, or staring into the knowing eyes of a horse.

I snap a picture of the cowboy hat before I give it back to TJ.

"All good, Doc?" TJ asks, straightening his own hat as he hangs the other one up.

I nod. "All good. You shouldn't need me for another six months, max. Unless you get a bumper crop of crias," I joke, referring to baby alpacas.

He shakes his head. "We're all done. But the missus wants you to have something she knitted from the herd—you got a few more minutes?"

"Of course." I grin and follow TJ to the house, where Sue presents me with a knit beanie.

"For those five days it gets cold enough to wear one," she says with a grin.

"It's awesome. So soft. Thank you!" I lean down to hug the shorter woman, no longer surprised at the incredible strength in her arms when she embraces me.

Back in my truck, I send Dawn a photo of the cowboy hat.

DAWN

I KNEW YOU WERE A COWBOY!

I laugh.

> Still not exactly a cowboy

You sent me a picture of a cowboy hat, James—what's a girl supposed to think? You're a cowboy. Admit it.

> Nope

I better see a cowboy hat at the masquerade ball.

> ...

Ooh, that means yes. That DEFINITELY means yes.

> It means maybe.

Maybe is yes.

> Maybe is not yes.

Yes it is.

> You're a maniac

A maniac who likes texting you, the cowboy. But I gotta go. Chat later?

> Of course.

xx

I sign off with another cowboy emoji, then head back to Lucky. Part of me feels a bit dishonest that I'm keeping the cowboy thing going, but I've read plenty of cowboy romances and I take care of large farm animals. Close enough.

Still, by the time I'm back at the clinic and have changed into a set of scrubs to see a few pets for the rest of the day, I'm a little freaked out. After sending Reid a text, I scoop Killer into the sling that Willa insisted I use and find Reid patrolling the town square.

"Hey!" I close the distance between us.

Reid nods, one hand absently scratching under Midnight's chin. "You finally succumbed to Willa's demand that you wear Killer?"

I tip my chin at the sling around him that holds the black cat. "Just trying to be as cool as you, Officer MacKinnon."

"Fuck off," he says good-naturedly. "What's got you so keyed up that you needed to come find me?"

"Dawn thinks I'm a cowboy."

He does a double-take. "Come again?"

I sigh and relay the situation, which, of course, he finds utterly hilarious.

"Wait—you sent her a picture of a horse?"

"That's what I said."

"And then," he laughs, "one of a cowboy hat?"

I cross my arms. "Reid. I've been telling you that for about five minutes, man. Are you gonna help me out or what?"

He keeps chuckling. "I don't know why it's so funny, but it's just..." he wipes a tear, "damn funny!"

"Is it, though?"

This makes him laugh harder.

I try a different approach. "C'mon, man. You lived in Miami. You're classy and I'm not."

Reid doubles over, tipping Midnight into the grass. "*I'm* classy? Wait till I tell Willa that's what you said about me. Even better—wait till I tell Ox!"

I make a noise of frustration. "You *can't* tell Ox."

But the dude just hits a button on his shoulder walkie-talkie thing and speaks into it. "Ox. Go to private."

"On it."

Reid flashes a grin.

I glare at him. "I hate you so much right now."

Ox's voice comes through the speaker. "Talk."

"Matty has this mystery woman thinking he's a cowboy, and now he's gotta dress like one at the masquerade ball later this week."

Immediately, the sound of laughter crackles through the radio. "Oh shit," Ox heaves, "that's amazing. *Matty?* A *cowboy?*"

"Okay, now you two are just being mean. Besides, I'm on farms half the week!" I protest.

All of this just makes them laugh harder.

"You know what? I'm leaving." I spin to leave, but Reid hustles around me.

"Wait, wait, wait," he says, a shit-eating grin on his face, "you gotta let us help."

"Let Reid help," comes Ox's voice. "I need to go."

I point at Reid. "You're not being helpful. You're being an asshole."

"That's fair. I'll behave. And you know I'm only giving you shit because I love you. But we really gotta get you suited up for this thing."

I groan. "That's why I came to you in the first place, man!"

He whips out his phone. "Is there, I don't know, a cowboy outfitter store around here?"

I gesture toward the beach. "You tell me, Reid. We're a beach town. What do you think?"

He points to my boots. "You're the one with cowboy boots." Then it hits him. "Wait. *You're the one with cowboy boots.* Holy shit, Matty—you *are* a cowboy!"

"Jesus fucking Christ."

In the end, I order a black cowboy hat from a store a few hours away that swears they can get it to me in time, and a black mask from Amazon. I half worry I'm going to look like a guy from an old black-and-white television show, but what can I do?

"One last thing." Reid holds a hand out to keep me from leaving.

I cut my eyes to him. "I'm hungry and I need to get home to let Kitty out."

"You need one of those giant belt buckles."

"Fuck you."

His cackles follow me all the way to my truck.

CHAPTER 10

GOLDIE

MY HANDS ARE shaking as I prop the phone up and FaceTime Willa. She answers almost immediately, and her eyes widen as she takes me in.

"What do you think?"

"Your hair!" Willa gasps.

"It's a wash." I wave her concern away. "Wanted to see how the other half lived." Instead of my usual blond tresses, I did a temporary brunette dye job. The color is much closer to what I think my hair might naturally look like, and it makes my blue eyes pop.

"Holy cow, Goldie," she breathes. "You're *stunning*."

I huff out a laugh. "As much as I blew on this outfit, I better."

I went totally against what I'd normally do. For an event like this, my instinct was to pick something in yellow. Instead, I'm in a dark blue satin number with a plunging neckline to below my breasts, that then falls in tight pleats to the ground. The back is a simple lace-up, leaving most of my skin exposed. It's simple, but gorgeous all the same. I've accessorized with black strappy sandals, black satin opera gloves that hide my typewriter wrist tattoo, and a lace mask.

"Hold on." I grab the mask and put it on, then twirl for her. "What do you think?"

"I think I wouldn't recognize you if I hadn't seen it for myself," she answers.

Good. It's exactly what I wanted. I can't explain it, but something tells me to hold back what I *really* look like just a little longer.

An alert from Blinding Love drops onto the front of the phone, blocking Willa's face from view.

"James just texted," I murmur, stepping forward to open it up.

"What's it say? He better not be canceling or I'll hunt him down and cut him."

I giggle. "Dang, Willa. Big sis don't play."

"Damn skippy."

Scanning the message, I tell her, "He's suggesting we have a code word."

Willa's face goes pink.

I narrow my eyes. "What's that look for?"

She presses her lips together. "Nothing."

"That's not nothing. Oh my God." Realization dawns. "This is something sexual with you and Reid, isn't it?"

She gets even redder, and I shake my head, laughing.

"Out with it," I demand.

"It's not the same," she protests. "We have a safe word, not a code word."

"A safe—Willa Dean *Dash*! Are you a," I lower my voice, though why I do it is anyone's guess, "*rope bunny*? How many kinks do you have?"

She covers her face. "We're not talking about my kinks."

I squeal. "Holy shit! I'm so impressed." I fan my face. "Hell, even *I* got a little hot thinking about that. Not about you two, good Lord, that's nauseating, but just, you know, generally."

She quirks a brow. "When was the last time you got laid?"

I hold up a finger. "Okay, first of all, we're not trying to get me all depressed right before what could be an amazing night. And secondly, look at you, talking about safe words and getting laid. Who even *are* you anymore?"

She laughs. "Whatever. Have fun. Be safe. And don't do anything I wouldn't do."

I pretend to consider this. "You know, it used to be that I would absolutely do the things you wouldn't do. But now? I don't know," I singsong.

"You're never letting this go, are you?"

"Never. Love you!" I blow her a kiss and disconnect.

BY THE TIME I GET OUT OF MY UBER AND TAKE IN THE swanky hotel on the fancy side of town, my stomach is in knots. What if all of this has been a gigantic ruse to kidnap me? And is 'kidnap' the word they use when adults are taken?

I shake my head and shut the thoughts down. I can't let myself go down this thought process or I'll be a complete disaster.

Or *more* of a disaster than I already am. Clearly.

"Miss?"

I startle and look up to find a man holding the hotel door open for me. "Yes?"

He smiles. "Would you like to come in?"

"Oh! Um, yes. Sorry. Thanks." I smooth my hands over my dress, grip my clutch like it's a weapon and I'm walking into a den of zombies, and move forward.

The ballroom is decked out like something from a fairytale. Thick curtains of cream and black are draped around the walls, and a small band plays jazz music in the corner. A disco ball turns slowly high in the air, sending sparkles of light around the room as it goes. Giant chandeliers are generously spaced, their crystals catching the ball's light and sending it back. People are everywhere, dressed in gorgeous gowns and fancy tuxedos.

I'm suddenly self-conscious in my simple blue gown, but at the same time, I can't fathom having worn something as elegant as what some of the women are dressed in.

I make a beeline for the bar, knowing I need a drink to calm my nerves. We'd said to meet at seven, but I made sure to get here nearly an hour ahead of time. No way was I going to let James see me before I saw him.

At the bar, I order a glass of white wine and turn to face the crowd, scanning to make sure I haven't missed him. He said he'd be in a cowboy hat, which, of course, made me smile like a total fool.

A couple on the floor catches my attention, and I look closer. The man is tall and broad-shouldered, and built like a tank. His dark auburn hair is tamed more than I've ever seen it, and in his arms is an absolute stunner of a woman. It's Ox…with a *woman*?

This night just got a lot more interesting. As I watch, Ox's hand slides down the woman's back possessively, then he pulls her close and presses a kiss to her lips. The whole thing is incredibly sensual, and it feels like I'm watching something I shouldn't. Clearing my throat, I take a sip of the cool wine and look away.

"Hey, Goldie."

I nearly jump out of my skin. "Ox?" Then, I look back at the dance floor and exhale a laugh. "That's Levi out there, isn't it?"

Ox grins. "It is."

"Wait." The blood drains from my face. "How did you know it was me?"

He winks behind his mask. "I'm just that good."

My eyes bug out. "Seriously?"

He nods. "No."

I swat his arm. "Asshole."

He laughs. "Your sister told me what you looked like. Otherwise I'd have no chance. You look beautiful," he says softly.

I grin. "Thanks, Ox. And you look very dashing yourself."

He looks down at the dark blue suit he's sporting. He really does look incredible, and I'm kind of mad at myself for not realizing it wasn't him on the floor out there. For one, Ox has a beard. "Thanks."

"Anyone here catch your eye?"

He gives a noncommittal shrug. "Maybe. And what about you? You're meeting someone, right?"

I swallow, nerves hitting me all over again. "Yes."

He nods, studying me. "Well, I'll be around if you need anything, yeah?"

"Thanks, Ox."

He takes his leave, and I glance at my watch. It's getting closer to when James will be here. My heartbeat kicks into overdrive.

Breathe, Goldie. You've got this. And hey, Ox is here. So if this goes sideways, he'll kick the guy's ass.

I take a deep breath and blow it out.

A few minutes later, I see a man who must be James enter the room, and my heart basically stops.

He's tall, but not too tall, and has a slim build. He's wearing the black cowboy hat, as promised, and a simple black mask. He begins to make his way to the bar, scanning the crowd as though he's looking for someone, and it allows me time to observe him a little more.

Something about him—his walk, maybe?—is familiar.

The closer he gets, the more I can't breathe. I shouldn't be this nervous. Why am I so freaking nervous?

And then he's near me, elbows resting softly on the bar as he faces one way while I'm still leaning with my back against the bar.

His scent. I know that scent.

Then he speaks. "Snuffleupagus walks alone."
Our eyes meet, and I nearly faint.
Because the man I'm staring at is Matthew Brodigan.

CHAPTER 11

GOLDIE

I BLINK. THEN I blink again. I'm not sure I'm breathing. But I *am* doing a fuck ton of blinking.

"Erhm, sorry." He clears his throat and starts to turn away. "I have the wrong person."

The thought of losing him is enough to launch me into action. "No!" I yelp, my mind racing. *What do I do? What do I do? Holy crap, what do I do?* Won't he know my voice? I'll change it. No idea how, but I'm doing it. I swallow, deciding if he recognizes my voice anyway, or anything else about me, then I'll admit it. Maybe he'll think this is funny. Like, ha-ha, what are the odds that you matched with your *best friend's little sister*, am I right? Hilarious! I clear my throat and make my voice a little deeper. "The crow flies at night."

His shoulders loosen and his mouth relaxes into a generous smile. "Dawn."

I finally allow myself to take a breath. "James."

"You look amazing," Matty says. The mask does nothing to dim his eyes. If anything, it makes them even more mesmerizing.

What was in that drink?

"Thank you," I smile, then gesture up. "Nice hat."

He chuckles, and the sound of it, low and sensual, sends shivers racing across my body. I swear I have never heard that sound come out of him, and it's doing funny things to my insides. He raises his fingers to the brim of it and tips it. "You like it?"

I nod. "The mask is a good touch."

It's a *great* touch. The damn thing is not only making his eyes look incredible, but also highlighting the fullness of his lips, and good gracious, he just *licked* them. I barely manage to repress a groan and an irritated stomp at the universe. Like, listen: I know he's hot. I've been acutely aware of this man's hotness—and goodness, and kindness, and goofiness, and loyalty—for literal *decades*. I do not need a dozen neon arrows blinking and pointing at him. I get it. I know.

And yet.

Even knowing all of this, I've never had the visceral reaction to him that I'm experiencing now. My palms are sweaty, for God's sake, and I can't wipe them on my dress because, you know, silk. It's fake silk, but still.

I turn to wave the bartender over, then glance back at Matty. "Drink?"

He grins. "Shouldn't I be the one asking you?"

I shrug. "I was here first."

He shifts closer and tilts his head toward me, and with the hat, the effect makes it feel like we're the only two around. When he speaks, his voice is low. "Oh, I noticed."

Is it hot in here? It's hot in here.

He straightens and orders our drinks. We're quiet while we wait, and when they come, he raises his in a toast. "To mysteries."

I can't help the smile that blooms on my face. "To mysteries."

We chat just as easily as if we were texting on the app, and when the lights dim even more and the band kicks into a slower song, Matty holds his hand out. "Shall we?"

I thread my gloved hand into his as my heart leaps into my throat. "I'd love to."

He pulls me close on the dance floor, leaving just enough room between us to keep it respectable. He smells so good, like always, dark vanilla mixed with laundry detergent. It's so distinctly Matty that I nearly blurt everything out, the scent of him luring me like a siren to my doom.

God, has he always had these muscles? And the cowboy hat—why is that so *sexy*?

"Talk to me, Dawn," he says, sending a fresh wave of shivers down my body. "You're awfully quiet now. Am I that bad of a dancer?"

I let out a nervous laugh. *If he only knew.* I remind myself to make my voice sound different. "Not at all. You're...wonderful," I finish.

He smiles, his hand tightening on mine while the other rests on my lower back like a branding iron. "Yeah?"

"Yeah," I say, breathier than I'd prefer.

"You smell amazing," he whispers. "It's familiar, but I can't figure out why."

Shit. It's my signature perfume, and surely, he's smelled it on me before. But he's never said anything, and why should he have? "It's, ah, a lot of things. You know, hair stuff, body wash, deodorant." Maybe I should stop dancing with him.

But it feels unbelievably good to be in his arms. And his breath on my neck is...

"Hmm?" he asks, pulling back to meet my eyes.

"What?"

A side of his mouth tugs up. "I thought you said something."

Nope. I suppressed a moan, Matty. God help me. "Just...thirsty. Maybe some water?"

"Of course. After you." His hand stays on my lower back as we move through the crowd and remains there when we get to the bar.

My blood is on fire. The water is a balm, but it does nothing to soothe the state this man has put me in. I'm barely able to keep my hands from shaking.

"So," he starts.

"So." I down the rest of the water and try to focus on anything that isn't Matty. The problem is that the man is wearing his suit like nature intended, complete with freshly shined boots and a shirt collar that's just tight enough around his neck to draw my attention. I swallow. There, just beneath his ear, is the freckle that I've always wanted to kiss.

I might combust.

"I—sorry." He glances away and laughs nervously. "You are— God, Dawn, you're taking my breath away here, and I still don't know who you really are. It's messing with my brain."

Oh, thank God. "Me, too," I confess. Minus the part where I don't know him, but you know, details.

"Can I just—" He stops. "Dance with me. I need—"

Fuck it. I grab his hand and lead him to the dance floor, pressing my body to his, threading a hand through the hair at the nape of his neck and wrapping my other arm around him. He shivers as he pulls me closer, one hand gripping my hip and the other splayed across my bare back. I suck in a breath. "Better?"

He nods, staring into my eyes. "Much."

If I thought I crushed on him before, then I'm a freaking goner now. The way he holds me, the way he's looking at me…this is not the Matty I'm used to. This Matty is oozing sex appeal and holds himself in a way that is both confident and desperate, as though he knows what he wants but isn't sure he'll get it.

And I will *so* let him have it. Consequences be damned.

I don't know how long we dance. It could be five minutes, it could be an hour. All I know is the heat of his hands against my skin, the silk of his hair, the broadness of his shoulders, and the sound of his laugh against my neck, velvet and deep. I never want it to end.

But end it does, when the band stops for a break. We make our way off the dance floor slowly, hands clasped, neither of us willing to let go of the other. Unfortunately, all the water and wine has had an effect, so I excuse myself to go to the restroom and make my way out of the ballroom and into a side hallway, finally finding the restrooms on the other side of another dark-ened ballroom.

As I wash my hands, I look at myself in the mirror. I don't recognize the woman staring back. It's not just my hair. Even my eyes look different with this mask, and my lips are stained a deep red, a color I never wear. It's no wonder that he doesn't recognize me.

I have no idea what I'm going to do. I should tell Matty it's me. I know I should.

But I can't. Not yet. It's selfish of me, but I can't bear the thought of him not looking at me the way he's looking at Dawn.

Tomorrow. I'll come clean tomorrow.

I dry my hands and leave the restroom, turning back to the ballroom when a hand darts out from the darkened room to my right and yanks me in.

I'm about to scream, but there's just enough light to see that it's Matty.

"Shh," he says.

"James," I breathe, proud of myself for not saying his real name.

He steps us farther into the dark, walking me backward until I'm pressed against a wall. My heart pounds and my mouth has gone desert dry. I watch silently as he moves, a shadow in the night, taking the hat off and placing it on a stack of chairs beside us.

"Can you see anything?" he asks.

"No," I whisper. My heart is about to pound out of my chest. I don't know what he's going to do, but I'm here for any of it. All of it.

Without a word, he removes his mask. I can't see his features, which is both a relief and a disappointment. His hands find mine, and I don't move as his fingers trail lightly up my arms and over the curve of my shoulders to my neck. Goosebumps trail in his wake, and I hitch a breath as his hands hover over the ribbon securing my mask.

He shifts closer. "May I?"

The only thing I can hear is my heartbeat. "Yes."

It takes only a moment for him to untie the ribbon and remove the mask. A second later, his hands are cupping my face and tilting my chin.

Fuck. I can't get enough air. My chest heaves.

He makes a noise in the back of his throat as his thumb strokes my skin. "So soft," he whispers. "I didn't let myself wonder what you looked like. I told myself it didn't matter. And it doesn't." He presses his thumb to my lower lip, dragging it down slowly, and it might be the sexiest thing I've ever experienced. He growls. "But these red lips, Dawn."

An ache blooms between my legs as my hands move of their own accord, finding the loops of his dress pants tugging him closer. I want to demand he kiss me. To beg. But I have no words. He's shredded them all with the ones he just uttered.

"May I kiss you?"

I squeeze my eyes shut in relief. "Please." It comes out as a whimper.

He threads his hand around the back of my neck, angling me exactly where he wants me, and then his lips lower to mine.

I moan as he takes my mouth, offering myself up on a platter. This man's words have already ruined me, and now his lips are killing me. I feel everything at once: his hands holding me in place, unbelievably strong and commanding, yet soft and gentle. The way his body surrounds and presses into mine exactly like I knew would happen. His scent invades me as his tongue licks across the seam of my lips and I open for him, knowing it was my last defense and unable to care.

When he groans, it unravels me. Teeth and tongues clash as his hand slides down the side of my body and dips into the open slit of the dress, his touch searing against my bare skin as he wraps his fingers around my thigh and pulls it up to anchor his hips between my legs.

We both curse at the contact, and he nips at my lower lip, pulling it into his mouth and sucking it before releasing it.

Without stopping the kiss, I push my hands up his chest, exploring the hard muscles obvious even beneath the dress shirt before moving one hand around and down to grab his ass and guide it forward. He rocks against me, the hardness of him doing little to ease my aching center.

"Dawn," he breathes, his chest heaving against mine. He starts to pull away. "We—"

"I know." I tug him back. I want to memorize everything about this moment. The darkness, the scent of him, the *feel* of him, the mystery that permeates all of it despite me knowing exactly who he is.

He kisses me harder, grabbing my wrists and raising my arms above my head to pin them against the wall as his mouth trails hot kisses down my neck. When his other hand grazes the side of my breast, I gasp, the sensation both too much and not nearly enough. His hand keeps going, the fingers tracing beneath my breast before falling to my stomach, then around to my waist to grip me hard.

"The things I would do to you, Dawn," he says, his voice low and dark. "We're not there yet, but when we are." He scrapes his teeth against my neck as he releases my arms, his lips soothing the light sting.

We stay there for a moment, just breathing, his head bent beside mine, before he reaches to grab my mask. Together, we position it on my face, and he ties it behind my head. In two short movements, he's secured his own mask and put his hat back on.

He reaches for me, his hand cupping my chin once more to place the lightest of kisses on my lips. "Can't wait to see if I ruined that lipstick." His chuckle is so signature *Matty* that I nearly crumple.

I place my hand in his and let him lead us back into the light. We pause at the edge of the ballroom. "How do I look?" I ask.

His eyes are soft, but his mouth tips into a wicked grin. "If I didn't know any better, I'd say you've been kissing someone." He closes the distance between us once more. "Dance with me."

We dance for another hour, until my feet are so numb I can't feel them. He walks outside with me to wait on an Uber, taking his jacket off and wrapping it around me when he sees me shiver.

Of course he does.

I blink up at him, wrapped in his scent and the warmth of his coat, and never want this night to end. When the car eventually comes, I return the jacket and get another kiss in return. Reluctantly, I get in the back seat, his scent still clinging to me as I turn to watch him. He holds his hand up, waving.

CHAPTER 12

MATTY

M Y HEAD IS spinning. All I can think is that I want more of her. God, her kisses. The way she just melted into me and let me completely take over. It was addictive.

I flop onto the couch, nowhere near tired despite the hour. And maybe I should leave her alone for the night, but I can't stop myself.

JAMES

> It's only been half an hour, but I want to see you again.

Her response is almost immediate.

> Me, too.

It's not just me. Thank God for that.

JAMES

> Apparently we've unlocked a video option, though.

Seriously?

Look in the upper right-hand corner. Click Options.

Holy shit.

My thoughts exactly.

Are you home? I'm home.

Crap maybe I shouldn't have told you that.

Killer hops onto the couch next to me, and I scratch his head before typing back.

Why, you afraid I'll use the timing to figure out where you live?

I live in Lucky.

I stare at the screen in disbelief, my thoughts whirring. She lives *here*? How do I not know who she is?

Could she be Goldie?

No. No way. The woman tonight looked nothing like her. *Sounded* nothing like her. Wasn't her.

Right?

God, but what if it was?

I shake my head and focus on Dawn. *Dawn. Dawn, Dawn, Dawn.*

Wait. Really?

Really.

This is big, Dawn.

I live in Lucky, too.

Yeah?

Yeah.

Anyway, yes, I'm home. Let my dogs out to do
their business and now I'm relaxing.

What are you wearing?

My dick twitches. All it takes are four little words, and apparently, I'm all the way in. Before I can answer, she's typing again.

You kissed me in a darkened room, James. Don't
get shy on me now.

I don't think *shy* is the issue.

JAMES
Are we really doing this?

It takes her a solid minute to answer, but I'm patient. Or terrified. Either way.

Yes.

Good. I think.

So tell me. What are you wearing?

I shift and stretch out on the couch, which Killer is not a fan of. "Sorry, buddy," I tell him. "You'd understand if you were, you know, human." I turn back to my phone to answer Dawn.

I've not changed. I'm still in my suit. But I did
take my boots off. You?

I'm in pajamas.

I let my head fall back and groan. Of course she is. I reach for every bit of bravery I have and type.

> Tell me what they look like.

> They're white with blue pinstripes. Button-down top.

> I want to see them. Not as a picture.

"Come on, go for the video," I whisper to my phone.

> You want to get on video?

"Yes!" I punch the air.

> Yes.

> No faces, though?

Frankly, I don't give a shit anymore. I am way too interested in this girl.

> Your call.

> No faces.

> Okay.

> Can you give me, like, five minutes?

I have no idea what she needs five minutes for, but whatever she wants.

> Of course. Just hit the button when you're ready.

Then it hits me. And I jump up to make sure I'm, you know, decent.

After the fastest manscaping in the history of manscaping, I've shut my bedroom door to keep the dogs and cats out and turned on the bedside light. I look at my bed, grateful I make it on the regular, and position the pillows against the headboard. My phone lights up with the video, so I launch myself onto the bed, shake off the nerves, and lean back against the pillows. I make sure the camera isn't pointing at my face.

"Hey," I answer. Then I croak, "Holy fuck."

She laughs. "So it was worth the five minute wait?"

"I'm staring at the most perfect pair of tits in the world, Dawn. It was absolutely worth the wait." It's clear she's wearing no bra, and they hang heavy behind a button-down that's a few shades away from sheer. If I stare hard—and I promise I am staring *really hard*—I can almost see her nipples. "Fuck," I breathe. "That's not fair."

"Unbutton your shirt." Her command is soft, tentative.

I sit up a little straighter. "Happy to." I look around. "Hang on, though—I need to figure out how to prop the phone up. Enjoy the view of my ceiling for a second."

Her answering laugh hits me in the chest as I toss the phone and look around for something to use. After a few moments of consideration, I grab the stack of romance books on my night-stand, then sit back on the bed with my legs spread in a V. I put the books between them. "Close your eyes a sec," I tell her, then position the phone so that my face isn't on screen. "Okay, open."

"Your shirt is still buttoned."

I grin. "I know." Then, thanking my lucky stars that I've read so many romance novels, I bring my hands on screen. I untuck the shirt first, then start with the button on top and unbutton slowly. "If I'd known a striptease was on the agenda for tonight, I'd have put an undershirt on," I tease.

She's quiet on the other end, but the view shifts just slightly, and I know she's still there.

"More?" I ask once I have the top three buttons undone. It's enough to where she can see a sliver of skin, but with the dim lighting in the room and the shadows of the fabric, she's not getting much just yet.

This is *fun*.

"More." Her voice is a whisper.

"Yes, ma'am." I move my hands to the next button, then the next, and the next. "All done," I say, but I make no move to do anything else.

She makes a noise of protest.

"Something wrong?" I ask, amused.

"Take it off," she whines.

I let my hands hover over the edges of the shirt. "I bet you can do better than that."

She takes a deep breath and lets it out, her breasts rising and falling as she does. I lick my lips, nearly able to taste the silk of her skin. "Take your shirt off, James." This time, her voice is authoritative.

"There we go." I peel the shirt off, and I don't miss the tiny moan she makes in response.

And I have never, so help me never, been more grateful for the time I spend wrangling farm animals and at the gym than I am right now. I decide to push more.

"Do you have any idea how much I want to kiss you again?"

She shifts on her bed.

"How much I'd love to take one of those perfect breasts in my mouth?"

"Oh my God," she breathes, squirming.

I unbutton my pants. Then I unzip them.

"James." Her voice is wondrous.

"Yes?"

"What are you doing?"

"How far are you willing to let me go, Dawn?"

She heaves a breath. "I—I don't know."

Slowly, I slide the tips of my fingers into my boxer briefs. "Is this good?"

She leans back against her pillows and raises her shirt, revealing a mouthwatering strip of golden skin.

I'm immediately hard. "Will you touch yourself for me?"

"You—you sound like you've done this before."

"Not even remotely. But I read."

Her hand rests at the waistband of her sleep shorts. "What do you read?"

"Romance."

"Really?"

"Really," I confirm. And God bless those authors. Otherwise, I'd have no idea how to do this.

"So, what would happen next if this was a romance book?"

"That's the beauty of romance books, Dawn. It's up to you."

Her fingers twitch. "What do you mean?"

"I mean," I start, then push my fingers into my briefs a little more, "that we go at your pace. We do what you want, no more, no less. We stop when you want." I pause. "Is that what you want? To stop?"

"No!" She nearly yells it, and it makes me laugh. "I mean, no. I just—this is new for me."

"Tell me what you want to do."

"I don't know," she answers softly. "Can I…"

"Can you what?" I urge.

She laughs nervously. "God, you can't even see my face, and I'm still so tongue-tied. Which is funny, because I thought I was a lot more, I don't know, *into* this. And I am, but I—" She moves her hands up, and when she speaks, it's muffled. "I want to watch you."

"You do? Naughty girl," I tease.

"See?" she groans into her hands. "You don't have to."

My answer is immediate. "I want to."

"You—you do?"

"Your wish is my command, Dawn."

"Oh," she breathes. "O-okay."

"But hang on. I'm going to take my pants off and then get back on screen."

"Whatever you want," she says, her voice high-pitched.

I hop off the bed and let my pants fall to the ground. *Am I really doing this?* Yes, apparently, I am. I don't recognize the person I am right now, but something about this woman brings it out in me. I'm back on the bed, still wearing my boxer briefs, in seconds.

"Hi," I say, getting situated once again and making sure the phone isn't capturing my face.

"Hi," she answers. "How does this work, exactly?"

I give a low laugh. "Pretty easily. Because I'm looking at your beautiful body, and I'm remembering what it felt like to feel your hot pussy against my cock." I slide my hand into my boxers and slide them down so she can see as I take myself in hand.

"Oh my God," she breathes. "That's so fucking hot." She moves, and it reveals another inch of skin.

I groan. "And I'm looking at that strip of skin above your shorts. I want to lick it, then take one of those nipples in my mouth, feel it grow taut against my lips." I pump myself slowly.

She puts her hand in her shorts.

"Fuck, Dawn. Are you going to get yourself off with me?"

"Uh-hmm," she whines softly.

"Tell me how wet you are."

"So wet already."

My mouth dries. "Show me."

She pulls her hand out and holds her fingers to the camera, where they glisten.

"Good girl," I grit out, pumping faster now.

"Holy shit, you just said good girl." She shoves her hand back into her shorts, gasping as her fingers make contact. "More. Talk more."

Whatever she wants. "You can see what I'm doing, Dawn, how hard I am for you. Are you playing with your clit?"

"Yes," she says on an inhale.

"Do you like it hard or soft? I want to know so that I'll do it right when it's my hand in there."

"Hard." Her knees come on screen, and she raises her hips.

"Fuck me, Dawn. Did you stick a finger in that sweet pussy?"

"Yes, holy—"

"Just one?" I grip myself hard, pumping the shaft and swirling the precum around my head.

"Two. Oh my God, so hot. So, *fuck*—" She cuts off and moans, her hips swiveling and tits bouncing. "So fast. I'm going to come," she whines.

"Come," I urge, feeling my own orgasm starting to build. "Don't you dare be quiet."

She isn't.

I watch, enraptured, as she brings herself to completion on the screen in front of me. The vision is seared into my mind for eternity, her hand down her shorts, her knees splayed wide, the skin of her stomach on display, the nightshirt bunched under breasts that are beyond perfect.

"Fuck!" I come with a roar, my own release catching me so off-guard that everything goes black for a second.

"Yes, God, *yes*, you're so fucking hot," she says as I release on my stomach.

We breathe, and it's almost like the aftermath of the kiss earlier tonight. As though we both need to gather ourselves. After a few moments, she slides her hand out of her shorts, and all I can think is how desperate I am to taste her.

I reach over to my nightstand and grab some tissues to clean myself up, then tuck myself into my boxers.

"That's a hell of a way to use the video function," I eventually say.

She laughs, loud and deep. "Yes, it is." Then she yawns. "Is it bad that I'm so tired?"

I grin. "No, because I am, too."

"You won't think any less of me if I say I want to go to sleep now?"

"Not even a little."

Her hand moves up, and I'm guessing it's to cover the massive yawn I hear. It ends in the most adorable squeak I've ever heard. "Talk tomorrow?"

I grin. She said *talk*, not *chat* or *text*. "Absolutely."

She disconnects and I lean over to turn the light off, then lie back with my hands under my head to stare at the ceiling.

I want more. Maybe it's time to tell her who I really am.

CHAPTER 13

GOLDIE

Fuck.

I just had video sex with my sister's best friend.

CHAPTER 14

MATTY

I WAKE UP to Killer licking my face, Kitty barking at something only he can see, and my cats yowling in protest. It's another day in paradise.

Except I need a minute to process what happened. Did I really do all those things last night with a woman whose face I still haven't seen?

What is *wrong* with me?

It's only now, in the light of day, that things feel much more real...and I feel much more off-kilter. This was a bad idea.

Maybe.

Was it?

Shit.

My phone dings. Maybe it's Dawn. I reach over to grab it, but it's Willa.

> **WILLA**
>
> Where are you? It's yoga and pier walk day. We're about to start. Are you sulking bc you can't bring Killer?

I run a hand over my face. There is no way I can do this today. None.

Sorry Wills, I can't pull it off today. Had a late night and overslept.

?? What'd you get up to last night?

Yeah, no way am I telling her. I'm still not sure that Reid's keeping his mouth shut, but her text makes it seem like maybe he is. Still...

Nothing. Just couldn't get to sleep.

I don't know if I believe you but okay. Call me later!

I let the phone drop to my chest. Killer decides now is a great time to get the zoomies on my bed, and proceeds to dart around the mattress like a dog possessed. A little maniac, but a cute little maniac.

He stops, looks at me, then does this adorable little bark-and-backward-scoot thing that definitely means he needs to go out.

I pull up the Blinding Love app and stare at the text chain with Dawn. Killer barks again. Finally, I type.

JAMES

Good morning

I'm an ass. Good morning? Is that all I have?

I don't get an answer immediately, but I'm not surprised. I'm not sure *I'd* respond to me if all I saw was "good morning." Groaning, I throw the covers off and get out of bed, with Killer zooming off the stairs leading down from the bed and scampering to the door to be let out.

I'm even less surprised when Reid shows up hours later, well after our normal yoga and pier walk would have happened. He bangs on the door like the cop that he is, causing way more of a ruckus than anyone needs to. "Open up! Police!"

I shush the dogs, then yank the door open and scowl at him. "Really?"

He smirks. "Works every time."

"You're an asshole."

"You're lucky I didn't bring Ox. Let me in."

I peek around him and see the squad car on the street. "You really want to get my neighbors' imaginations going with the car, don't you?"

"Do I need to radio Ox?"

"Does the chief of police work on Sundays?"

He shrugs. "Maybe, maybe not."

I sigh and step aside. "Come on in. Want some coffee?"

He smiles broadly. "Why thank you. Yes I would. Can I let Midnight down?" He gestures at the sling across his bulletproof vest.

"If I said no, you'd do it anyway."

He shoulder-checks me as he walks in. "That's true."

"If my pets lose their shit, I'm not taking responsibility," I warn, then lead the way to my kitchen.

Once he has his cup of coffee, he leans against the counter and studies me. "So?"

"So…what?"

He snorts. "Don't be obtuse. How did it go?"

"That's an awfully big word for a cop," I tease, hoping to keep him at bay and knowing perfectly well that it isn't going to work.

It doesn't.

"It was…incredible."

Reid smiles. "Yeah?"

"Yeah," I confirm, my own smile growing. "It really was. She's amazing. Funny, and gorgeous—"

"You saw her face?"

My neck heats. "I saw enough."

"What's with the weirdness?"

"I'm not being weird."

He tilts his head. "You're definitely being weird."

"No, I'm not."

"Yes, you are."

"Am not."

"Are too."

"I'm not, and even if I were, I don't want to talk about it yet. But I'm not, so there's nothing to say."

Reid's eyes narrow as he takes a long, loud slurp of his coffee. "I don't like this." He gestures at me. "You, that is. The coffee's great. But something is off and you're not telling me."

I push off the counter. "Listen. The night was amazing. Really. We danced, we talked, we laughed, we had a great time."

"Can I tell Willa?"

"No!"

He shakes his head. "See? Something's weird. If you're not going to tell me, you should at least tell your best friend."

Yeah, that is not happening. I can only imagine how that would go.

Hey, Willa, funny story. I've been talking to someone over an app, but I don't really know who she is. She and I finally met at a masquerade ball, and we made out in a dark room, and it was hot as fuck. Then we went to our own homes, logged on to a video chat, and watched each other get off. Oh, and I still don't know what she looks like. And I'm positive her name isn't Dawn, because she also told me she lives in Lucky and I don't know any Dawns. And maybe it's your baby sister, but it can't possibly be, but what if it is and I saw her orgasm. Anyway, yeah. Cool?

No way. "Thanks for your insight, Officer."

"Fine. Have it your way."

I smile, relieved.

"But I'm drinking all your coffee." He stalks to the coffee pot.

I pull my phone out and open the app. Still nothing.

I've definitely messed this up.

CHAPTER 15

GOLDIE

I STARE AT the text.

Is he serious right now? Good morning? Good *morning?* Is that literally all the man is sending? We watched each other fuck ourselves with our hands last night and all he has to say in the light of day is *Good morning?*

What am I supposed to do with that?

Did we go too far, too fast?

Yes.

Yes, we clearly did.

Also, he doesn't even know who I am—despite me knowing *very* much who he is.

Who knew that little Matty Brodigan would grow up to be, well, *not*-little Matty Brodigan? Holy crap, I'm getting worked up just remembering how ridiculously thick his dick was.

Is. How thick his dick *is.*

And the second he realizes it was me on the other side? What then?

I am so screwed.

Wait. It's Sunday. It's yoga-and-walk-on-the-pier Sunday. With that realization, I'm up and moving. I screech into the yoga studio with a literal minute to spare, but only Willa and Reid are there. No Matty.

"Where's Matty?"

Reid shoots me a curious glance while Willa answers, "Says he wasn't up to it this morning."

I try hard to keep my expression neutral. "Too bad. Hope he's feeling okay." Is that what I would normally have said? I have no idea anymore.

"What's with the hair?" Reid asks.

I shrug. "Felt like experimenting. I'm washing it out later." Also, holy *shit*. I can't believe I didn't think about my freaking hair. What if Matty had been here? He would have known. Instantly.

"If the chatterboxes in the back could be quiet," the teacher says from the front.

My cheeks heat with the admonishment, but at least I don't have to talk anymore. I start the sun salutation that most people are halfway through and try to lose myself in the session.

Ninety minutes and more holding of poses than I was even remotely ready for later, my body is loose but my mind is in free fall. What have I done?

Good morning. *Good morning?*

I can't get past it. What else could he have said? I don't know, but was 'good morning' with no punctuation the way to go? No!

But also, did I respond? No, because…ugh, because I had video sex with *Matty fucking Brodigan* and he's my sister's best friend and what am I going to do?

Cool, I'm spiraling again.

I can't hide the flinch when Willa touches my elbow.

She narrows her eyes and leans close, tucking her mat under her arm. "How did last night go?"

"Oh! Um…good."

She looks over to Reid, who's scooping Midnight into the sling and chatting amiably with a gaggle of women. I have no idea how Willa manages not to seethe with jealousy constantly. I'd probably go all Terminator on them, but clearly that's just me. She swings her gaze back to me. "Just good? Really?"

"It was good." I double down. "You haven't—you haven't told Reid, right?"

"You asked me not to, and I haven't. Promise." She holds her hand up. "Sisters before misters and all that. Even though I don't understand the secrecy."

I breathe a little easier. I can't explain why I feel the need to keep this quiet, but I do. "Thanks." I start heading to the front.

"But I want to know more about last night. *Way* more," she whispers.

"Feel like a late brunch since Matty isn't here to walk the pier?" Reid asks. "I'm feeling noshy."

I snort. "Noshy? What are you, eighty?"

"And to think, I was going to pay for you, but now..." He trails off and smirks. "Mimosas are on you. Diner?"

What if Matty is there? Thinking fast, I toss out, "How about somewhere else? Maybe that breakfast place outside of town?"

"Ooh, yes!" Willa's eyes light up. "I've been wanting to try their Eggs Benedict. Someone said their Hollandaise was better than mine."

"Impossible." Reid pulls her to him and kisses her temple.

My heart squeezes. I'd never be jealous of my sister, but if I'm being honest, I really thought I would have been the one to find her happily ever after first. Is that bad of me? "Meet you there," I tell them.

I give myself a pep talk before I go into the restaurant. I can do this. All I have to do is remain calm, cool, and collected. Maintain eye contact as needed, but don't overdo it. Avoid thinking about Matty and the way he kissed me. And *definitely* avoid thinking about his thick dick.

I groan and lay my head on the steering wheel.

Inside, I join Reid and Willa at a corner booth, with Reid on the outside and facing the front door, as always. I've known people who prefer to have a view of the front door, but for Reid, it's more than a preference. He absolutely *must* be able to see what's going on at all times. He says it's standard police stuff, but I think it goes back to all that mess he got into with the Bunnies.

Willa and I each get mimosas, and I get the breakfast tacos. Willa orders the Eggs Benedict, of course, and Reid orders a burger and iced tea.

"What did you get up to last night?" Reid asks. "I heard there was some fundraiser thing at the pricey hotel."

My heart plummets into my stomach. "Oh?" I stammer, reaching for the mimosa and taking a deep swallow. "I just hung out at home."

Willa looks at him. "How did you know about the masquerade ball?"

Reid shrugs. "Ox mentioned it. Said his brother was swinging in for it and bringing Charlotte with him and everything." He glances back at me. "You really didn't hear about it?"

He knows. He has to know.

"Nope!" It comes out like a chirp.

He regards me silently, his face as blank as a master poker player.

He definitely knows. Does that mean Matty knows?

Oh, *God*.

Does Matty know it's me? If he does, then why didn't he say anything?

Does Reid *know*? Like, *know* know?

Wait. Does *Willa* know? Crap. What if Willa knows and she's staying quiet out of some best friend loyalty?

But doesn't sisterhood trump best friends?

I'm spiraling. Again.

I take another gulp of the mimosa and wave the remainder at the server. I'm definitely gonna need another. Or three.

Willa, bless her, changes the subject, and when the food

comes, I dive in so that I have something to do that doesn't involve hoping against hope that Reid hasn't already figured me out.

Damn cops.

"This isn't as good as mine," Willa declares. "It's not nearly as thick and creamy."

"I've got something thick and creamy for you," Reid jokes.

"Okay, *ew*," I gag. "Stop that. Stop that right now."

Willa laughs. "Looks like you found Goldie's line."

"That should be *everyone's* line," I protest. "Do not ever talk like that in my presence again."

Reid laughs and pops a fry in his mouth. "You got it, Goldie."

After a mere two mimosas and some delicious tacos that I have to repeatedly assure Willa are not, in fact, as good as hers, we wrap it up and get ready to leave. Willa holds me back while Reid goes to the front to pay.

"What is going on?" she asks. "You were distracted and barely talking the whole time. Usually, we can't shut you up."

"Maybe it was Reid's nasty mention—"

"Nope," she cuts me off. "Nice try, though. What happened last night? Was he an asshole? Did he smell? Oh my God!" She grips my arm and yanks me to her, lowering her voice. "Did he try something? Does that asshole not know what the word 'no' means? I will sic Reid on him so fast."

I can't help the giggle that comes out. "Easy there, killer. He wasn't an asshole, he didn't stink, and anything that happened was done with my enthusiastic consent."

She whirls on me. "I *knew* it! Did you kiss? Did you take your masks off? What does he look like?"

"Yes, yes, and I don't know."

She raises a brow. "Come again?"

I'd like to, very much, thank you.

I shake my head. I need to focus. I take a deep breath and meet her eyes. "Fine. I'm giving you this because I know I was an insane person when you and Reid were just getting together.”

“Glad you can finally admit that. Now spill. But hurry, because Reid’s waiting.”

I look and sure enough, he’s paid and is waiting on us. “Fine. He took our masks off in the dark, we kissed, I didn’t see his face, and it was the hottest thing I’ve ever experienced.”

She squeals and grabs my arms. “*Goldie!* Seriously?”

“Calm down.” I widen my eyes and look around. “*Please.*”

“But this is so *exciting*! What if he’s the one? Oh my gosh, we could have double dates and hang out at each other’s houses, and the guys could do guy things and…” She sighs happily.

I might puke. And it has nothing to do with the mimosas.

Grabbing my phone, I look at the screen and pretend there’s a text from JJ. “Oh, look at that. I need to go, sis. Work calls!”

“On a Sunday?”

I pull her into a hug. “News never sleeps. Love you.”

Reid gets the same spiel on my way out, too.

“Let me drive you to the office, then,” he says. “I’ve got to start my shift soon anyway.”

“Nope!” I answer brightly and swivel away from him. “I’ll be just fine.”

“Wait.”

His commanding voice stops me in my tracks.

Reid continues, advancing on me in full police officer mode. “How many drinks did you have in there?”

I roll my eyes. “Two mimosas, *Officer MacKinnon*. And they were skimping on the champagne, I assure you.”

He’s unconvinced. “It’s field sobriety test time, Miss Dash. Follow my finger.”

“Willa, your boyfriend is being mean!” I call out, laughing as I dutifully follow Reid’s finger.

“Wouldn’t be the first time,” she responds.

“Walk nine heel-to-toe steps in a straight line,” Reid intones.

I obey, then turn and walk back nine steps at his direction, too. When he makes me stand on one leg with the other raised off the ground, I do it, only objecting when he tells me to count by thousands.

"Reid!" I huff out, exasperated and still holding my foot up. "Let me go already."

"Fine. But text your sister when you get to the office."

I promise, and then I bolt.

CHAPTER 16

MATTY

KILLER'S BLADDER IS the size of a pea. *Maybe* a chickpea, if I'm being generous.

At this point, that's my professional opinion.

I let him into the backyard, and after a quick trip, he's back, dancing at my feet and wanting nothing more than to be picked up.

Scooping him into my arms, I check my phone. Now that five a.m. seems to be my new wake-up time, I can see that Dawn didn't respond overnight. Or at all yesterday.

I knew my *Good morning* text was bad, but was it *that* bad?

Apparently.

I read back through our texts, stunned at the amount of frankness we've given each other, despite not giving each other a lot of facts about ourselves.

I put Killer down to sniff around the kitchen, then decide to put my metaphorical big boy pants on and try again.

JAMES

> Are you feeling as weird about the other night as I am? Because I've gotta tell you, I'm freaked out. Doing something like that was unbelievably hot.

> But also…we don't know who each other is. Not really.

> All this to say that I'm a little freaked, but also, I still like you. And I still want to talk to you, if that's something you want.

I take a deep breath. Being vulnerable over text is no easier than doing it in person. But I owe it to her, and to me, to do it. Besides, if I'm trying to be less boring, then surely this is helpful.

I shake my arms out. I can do this.

One thing, though.

> If we're going to keep doing this, I think it's time to start telling each other the truth.

> Not that I've been untruthful exactly, but there are things about me that I've definitely withheld out of a desire to be safe. And I don't want to be safe with you anymore.

The ball is in your court, Dawn.

I hope I hear back from you.

It's all I can do. I turn the screen off and let Killer back outside, this time with Kitty. They can tend to their business while I put on some workout clothes. After that, it's feeding time for them, the cats, and Hedgie, and then I head to the gym.

Later at the clinic, Killer settles happily into his little nest of blankets behind Liv's desk, snuffling under the pile until all we eventually see is the tiniest strip of cream-colored head.

"He's too cute for words," Liv says. "How did you get the only nice chihuahua I've ever met?"

"Hey, there are no bad dogs—only bad owners," I say in my best veterinarian voice. Then I smile. "No clue, though. I got lucky, I suppose."

"Well, Mr. Lucky," Liv turns to the computer screen and studies it, "you have a lot of patients today. Hope you brought lunch."

I did, but by the end of the day, the paltry peanut butter and jelly sandwich has long gone. Even worse, I've heard exactly nothing from Dawn, so it's definitely a dinner at Dash In Diner kind of night. They've started staying open longer now that Willa is in charge, and of course, business is booming. I tuck Killer into the sling around my chest, fully aware that I look ridiculous, but I'm covered in pet hair anyway. What's a little three-pound dog on top of it?

I make my way to the packed diner and slide onto the last open stool at the counter. Willa smiles at me through the window, and a little later, she comes out to give me a hug. Naturally, she sees right through my paltry excuse for a smile, and levels the same look on me that's worked for decades.

"What's wrong?" She doesn't take her eyes off mine as she gives Killer a scratch behind his big ears.

Resisting the urge to squirm, I say, "It's nothing for you to worry about."

When I don't say anything else, she hollers at their other line cook, Jake. "I'm taking five. You got it handled back there?"

When he answers in the affirmative, she jerks her head to the door. "Come on. Outside."

Wordlessly, I follow her out of the diner and sit on one of the wooden benches framing the entrance. "Willa—"

"No," she cuts me off. "Don't 'Willa' me. You've been weird for a couple of weeks now. You're hiding something from me. What's going on?"

I scrub my face and sigh. "It's complicated."

"And when has that ever stopped you from talking to me? Need I remind you about the underground kitten ring you ran in elementary school?"

I quirk a smile. "Okay, but they were so cute, and there were just so many of them."

She leans into me. "Talk to me, bestie."

But I still hesitate. "I'm not ready to talk about it," I admit. She stiffens, and I put my arm around her to pull her to me. "Don't be mad. I'll tell you, I promise. But I'm still trying to figure things out, and I want to do it on my own."

She looks at me. "Since when have you done things on your own? You're a pack animal, Matty."

She's not wrong. and yet, for some wild reason, I feel like this is one time where I'd do better talking to Goldie instead of Willa. I'm not calling her, but the instinct hits me like a ton of bricks.

Unless Dawn is Goldie.

I still can't quite shake the notion, because it would make so much sense if it were her. The ease we have in talking to each other, for one. But it's not her—it can't be. The woman I was with at the masquerade ball wasn't Goldie. Those lush lips, the way they parted for me…no way. Not to mention what we did afterwards. Jesus. If I had video sex with my best friend's *little sister?*

No.

Willa stands abruptly. "Fine. Don't talk. But if whatever this is blows up in your face, I don't want to hear it." She yanks open the door.

"Wait." I gesture her back to the bench, unable to let her leave with her feelings hurt. "It's about a girl."

"I *knew* it!" She's far too satisfied with the answer as she sits back down.

"Yeah, well, don't get too high and mighty with me. I think it's over."

She frowns. "Why?"

"It's…complicated."

She snorts. "You said that already. And of course it is."

I pet Killer. "What do you mean?"

"Because you're one of the most sensitive people I know. You are a walking, talking golden retriever. Aren't you the one who reads all the romance novels?"

"Yeah. So?"

She leans into me. "*So*, don't you think you can figure this out? What would the dude in one of your novels do?"

I can't help but laugh. "I don't know, Willa. I'm pretty sure I'm more like the women in the novels than the men."

She eyes my cowboy boots. "You sure about that?"

I shove back against her. "Shut up."

She laughs. "I'm just saying. I know *we've* never been like that, but you're a good-looking guy. You've just spent your whole life with your nose in books, then with your arms way too far up in cow business to notice that plenty of women are interested."

I scoff and look around. "Where are these women you speak of?"

"Listen, if *my* oblivious ass can see them, then you know they're around."

"No. I'm the boring guy that no one thinks about."

Willa raises an eyebrow. "I beg to differ."

"Differ all you want, but the proof is in the pudding."

She stands again. "I'm not arguing about this. You're wrong, and that's the end of it."

I laugh again as I rise and pull her into a hug. "You smell like fries."

"I always smell like fries, asshole. I need to get back in there." She pulls back and points a finger at me. "I'm ready to listen when you're ready to talk."

"Love you, Willa."

"Love you, too."

She disappears and I take a minute before going back inside, curiosity gnawing at me. *Who is Dawn?* How have I never seen her around, and never talked to her or heard her name before all this started? There's something I'm missing, and it's as though it's just off-screen and out of view.

A flash of blue hits my periphery as Reid rounds the corner and heads my way. Defeated, I drop my head into my hands and fall back onto the bench as he approaches. "Officer MacKinnon," I mutter through my hands. "Of fucking course." Because I can't catch a break in any capacity.

He gestures at my splayed form on the bench. "Do I need to arrest you for something, Matty?"

"Not unless there's a new law about irritating your best friend because you won't tell her about your dating life. Or lack thereof."

He laughs and eases onto the bench, taking Willa's spot and giving Killer a cursory pat. The little dog licks his hand in response. "Remind me why you're not telling her again?"

"Apparently, because I'm an idiot."

He snorts. "She's not wrong."

"She didn't say I was an idiot. She called me a golden retriever."

He gives me a confused look.

"Listen, being a golden retriever is good. Most of the time."

He still doesn't speak.

I sigh. "Fine. She didn't call me an idiot, but it was heavily implied."

He grins and pats my back. "Come on. I'll buy you a shake."

"What am I, twelve?"

"No, but you look like you could use a shake. Chocolate? Or are you one of those weird people who like strawberry?"

"I think *you* could use one and I'm your foil. And strawberry is good."

He opens the door and I walk ahead. "Strawberry is not good. If you get that, I'm not buying."

Reid absolutely buys me the strawberry shake, but only after loudly proclaiming his dislike for it to the entire diner. To my credit, I keep from checking my phone the entire time we're eating.

Which is for the best, because there's no response from Dawn when I get home, and none by the time I finally drift off to sleep.

It's over. And honestly? It sucks.

CHAPTER 17

GOLDIE

MATTY'S MESSAGES ARE haunting me. It practically melted my phone all day yesterday, and even JJ noticed I was staring at my screen more than usual. Of course, his gossip antenna went up, but I kept him at bay.

I don't know what to do, and I need to talk to someone. I can't talk to Willa. Or Reid. Ox might actually be an option, but that feels weird, too.

Mom and Dad are out. Like, *way* out.

That leaves Agatha.

And isn't that something?

I'm knocking on her door before I can think twice.

"Goldie!" She smiles wide as she opens the screen door to let me in. "To what do I owe the pleasure of an early-morning visit? Have you reconsidered my offer to set you up with someone? Because I just got word of a new man in town. He's in his forties, but—"

"I'm kind of involved with Matty Brodigan but he doesn't know it's me and we made out in a dark room at the masquerade ball and did some other things later and now I think I need to tell him it's me but I'm scared and I need help."

Agatha blinks.

I blow out a breath and smile like a maniac. "Help?"

The old woman doesn't miss a beat, smiling brightly and stepping back to wave me in. "Well, it seems we have some work to do!"

In moments, she's got me seated at her kitchen table with some coffee and a slice of lemon poppyseed bread.

"I think you should start at the beginning. Leave nothing"— she touches my arm— "and I mean *nothing* out."

I raise an eyebrow. "I'm not sure you're ready for that."

She laughs. "Dear, have you bothered to do the math on me? I was in my twenties in the sixties. You've heard of that decade, right? The one called the *sexual revolution?*" She titters and brings her cup to her mouth for a sip. "You kids these days think you're the first generation to have orgies. I swear."

I nearly choke on my coffee. *Orgies?* Holy shit.

"Agatha!"

She shrugs primly. "See? You're shocked." She sets her cup down. "Get over yourself and tell me the story."

So I do. After a moment. Because I need to, well, get over myself. I tell her everything: signing up for the app a year ago, hearing nothing, the initial outreach and decision on both our parts to keep the mystery going, my shock at realizing it was him at the ball, changing my voice, the make-out session, the orgasm session, and so on.

"What do I do?"

"You come clean. Tell him it's you."

I gape at her. "But—"

She waves my protest away. "Goldie. What do you have to lose?"

"Everything!" I sputter. "I have everything to lose!"

She tilts her head and regards me. "Okay, but what do you have right now?"

Oh. "Nothing." The word is soft as I speak.

Agatha keeps going. "Do you think it might be worth the risk?" She takes another sip of coffee and regards me. "Besides, can you really go the rest of your life looking at Matty and knowing it was the two of you this whole time? What happens when he finds someone else?"

A sense of irrational possession and jealousy spears through me. Fuck that. *Fuck that.*

"You're right."

She looks at my phone, then at me. "So?"

I pull the phone toward me and click on the app, then navigate to the messages. His last words stare back at me.

> If we're going to keep doing this, I think it's time to start telling each other the truth.

> Not that I've been untruthful exactly, but there are things about me that I've definitely withheld out of a desire to be safe. And I don't want to be safe with you anymore.

> The ball is in your court, Dawn.

> I hope I hear back from you.

"Am I doing this?" I ask Agatha.

"Yes." Her tone brooks no argument. Leave it to me to get the best advice from a seventy-something.

DAWN

> I'm sorry I haven't replied. I've been entirely freaked out, too. But I'm ready to tell you everything. To start, I already know who you are.

> Who you really are.

> I knew who you were the second I saw you at the Ball.

The dots on Matty's side almost immediately start up. I squeal and drop the phone. Agatha looks over to read it, too.

JAMES

You know my name?

You're Matty Brodigan.

How'd you know?

Biting my lip and looking at Agatha, I decide to be truthful.

Your boots were a dead giveaway. And your eyes.

Seconds pass.

A minute.

Agatha groans in frustration. "What's with the little dots?"

"It means he's typing a response."

"Well, what's the hold-up? Is the man typing one-handed?"

I laugh. "Welcome to the wonderful world of online dating, Agatha. It's brutal."

She sniffs. "If it weren't Matty on the other end, I'd be figuring out another man to set you up with."

"Don't you dare," I warn her.

She points at the screen. "He answered!"

I feel like I should apologize, because if you know me, then it seems I should know you, right?

"Tell him," Agatha says.

"No way," I answer. "Not over the app."

You know me, but there's a good reason you didn't recognize me.

So...what now?

Agatha shakes my arm. "You have to meet him."

"I know. But this is…hard."

She scoffs. "Of course it's hard. Why do young people think love is going to be a breeze?" She points to my phone. "You set up a time to meet him right now, young lady, or so help me, I'll call JJ right now with the scoop of his life."

My eyes widen. "You wouldn't dare."

Hers narrow. "Try me, missy."

I gasp. "Rude."

"Start typing."

I study her. "You know, you both inspire and terrify me." But I do as she instructs.

> Let's meet. Hall's Balls. Tonight at eight. I'll be the girl at the bar in yellow.

There's a beat where he doesn't type at all.

I want to puke. "Oh, God. Was the yellow a giveaway?"

Agatha rolls her eyes. "Don't be so dramatic. He's deciding what he'll wear." She points at the phone. "See? He's typing."

> I'll be the guy in the cowboy boots. 😉

I'm not proud of the noise that comes out of me. Or the fantasies I immediately start having. Like how he sees it's me and twirls me around, a big smile on his face, before laying another one of those hot-as-sin kisses on me. Like how he's not at all worried about telling my sister and parents. Like he doesn't care about the gossip that will inevitably spread about us.

Agatha looks at me, as satisfied as a cat in sunshine. "Told you."

CHAPTER 18

MATTY

I SHOULDN'T BE as nervous as I am. She knows me. She *knows* me.

She knew who I was when we…did what we did…and I have never been self-conscious about sex or myself, but suddenly I am.

It's not embarrassing, exactly, but it's unnerving. Like she had an unfair advantage.

The thing is…I think I know who it is. Who *she* is. Despite all logic. Despite a long-buried, un-inspected wish.

Regardless of whether it's her or not, I'm still getting there an hour ahead. She had me beat the last time we met, and now, it's my turn.

I wear my cowboy boots, as promised, along with my favorite jeans and a dark teal T-shirt that Willa always says makes my eyes 'pop,' whatever that means. I feed Hedgie and the dogs, then crate Killer with his favorite stuffed lamb before heading to the bar.

Anthony is behind the bar as always. He uncaps my favorite beer, a pilsner from the brewery in town, without me so much as asking, and it's sliding into my hand as I ease onto the stool.

"By yourself?"

"Meeting someone."

He nods and turns away without another word. I bite my cheek to keep from laughing. The man couldn't be more different from his gossip-mongering brother if he tried.

I take a swig of the beer. And another, and another, until it's gone and Anthony is sliding another in front of me. I'm halfway through it when a flash of yellow in my periphery has me turning.

My vision narrows to pinpoints, and everything else gets blurry. I grip the glass like it's going to keep me from drowning.

A faint humming sounds in my ears, and it's impossible to think as I scan her head to toe, the entire world grinding to a halt as I try to make sense of the woman in front of me. I open my mouth, but nothing comes out. I can't speak. My brain is malfunctioning. I've glitched.

Goldie Dash.

The woman I suspected, but didn't dare hope for.

Looking at me as though she's in trouble and biting her lip. A lip I've tasted.

"You," I croak.

She nods wordlessly.

I force my jaw shut and swallow thickly. "Holy shit."

She perches on the stool next to me, one foot resting on its rung and the other tipped on the floor, clearly ready to bolt at the slightest misstep as my life flashes in front of me.

Goldie running to catch up with me and Willa. Goldie building sandcastles with us on the beach. Goldie's hand as we walked home, pudgy and sticky in mine after too many popsicles. Goldie in middle school, Goldie as a sophomore when we were seniors. Goldie here. Goldie there. Goldie everywhere.

Goldie. *Goldie.*

Reality is crashing over me in waves as I stare at her. Is this okay? Am *I* okay?

Oh, God. I've *seen* her. And she's *seen* me.

It was the hottest night of my life.

With my best friend's little sister.

It's a freaking trope from a romance novel. I've read this book before. Only this is real fucking life. *My* life.

"You," I breathe again. "Your hair."

"Temporary wash."

"Your tattoo."

"Covered by the gloves.

"Your voice."

"Easily changed," she says, sounding like Dawn.

"And your scent," I whisper.

Her lips curve. "Didn't change."

I nod, everything locking into place. Of course it was her. How could it have been anyone *but* her?

She remains quiet, meeting my gaze unflinchingly.

Anthony saunters over. "Tito's and water with a lime?"

She startles at his gruff voice. "Please." When his back turns, she mutters, "I'm gonna need it."

A soft, disbelieving laugh escapes me as her eyes lift back to mine.

CHAPTER 19

GOLDIE

"**A**RE YOU OKAY?**"** It's the only thing I can think to say.

"I...don't know. I think so." His cheeks are a little pink.

I'm overcome with the need to touch him.

Which is probably the worst idea ever.

"Drink." Anthony tosses a napkin in front of me and sets the drink on top.

I snatch it and take two massive gulps, then proceed to cough. "Heavy...pour," I gasp, thwacking my chest as I struggle to get myself back under control.

Happily, the whole thing has served to yank Matty out of his daze. He jerks to attention, grabbing my left arm and pulling it into the air.

The move is so startling that I look up at him, lightly coughing as I ask, "What...are...you doing?"

"My grandma always said to raise your left arm when you coughed." His cheeks get even rosier as he releases my arm and resettles on the stool. "Sorry."

A pint glass of plain water appears as Anthony glares at me. "Water."

I do as he says, sipping at the water until I get myself under control. Or as under control as possible, given that Matty is still studying me with an intensity I can barely take.

His eyes. The slight furrow between them. The way he's biting the inside of his cheek. All of it makes me press my legs together to try and ease the ache there.

After another few minutes of silence, I finally cave. "Are you going to speak at all?"

He clears his throat and takes a sip of the fresh beer Anthony slid in front of him. "You've had a lot longer to come to grips with this than me."

The word *grip* makes me think of the way his hand wrapped around his dick, and my cheeks heat. "Fair."

He blows out a breath, then reaches to touch a strand of my hair. "You...dyed it just for the one night?"

It takes everything not to lean into his touch. "I put a temp wash on it," I explain. "I don't know why. But I did. Do you— would you have recognized me otherwise?"

"Honestly? I'd like to think so, but..." He trails off as his eyes search my face, spending more time on my lips than is decent. I lick them self-consciously, and I swear to God, a tiny moan escapes him. A moan that I've only heard two other times. "Stop," I whisper.

Matty's gaze snaps to mine. "Stop what?"

I shake my head, leaning forward to whisper. "Stop staring at my lips and moaning, because I've freaking seen your dick, Matthew, and right now? All I want to do is take you into the bathroom and go to my knees. So. *Stop.*"

His jaw unhinges. "Holy..."

I straighten and fluff my hair. "I said what I said."

He chuckles, then it grows into a laugh. A deep belly laugh. Which makes me start laughing, until we're both practically howling, tears streaming down our faces. "You said...what you said," he sputters, then we laugh again.

Finally, we ease out of laughing, and I wipe the tears away. As we reach for our drinks, our eyes meet and hold. They hold as we drink and stay connected as we set our glasses on the bar. I want to fall into their caramel swirls forever.

"What are we going to do?" he whispers.

I press my lips together and shake my head, unable to answer him. Because it hits me that maybe he might want this. But maybe he doesn't. That despite our weeks of getting to know each other as James and Dawn, it might not be enough. Maybe the only thing I'll ever be to him is his best friend's little sister.

He looks up at Anthony, who's moved down to our end of the bar to check on us. "I think we need shots. Yes?" He glances at me.

"Yes." I can't say it fast enough.

"Tequila?"

"Again, yes."

Anthony swivels his gaze between the two of us, probably trying to assess what's going on. The good thing is, even if he were to somehow figure it out, he won't tell his brother. And right now, I think we both need as much privacy as this town will give us. He must get whatever he's looking for, because he nods and turns away to grab the bottle and shot glasses.

"Don't bother with salt and lime," I tell him, my eyes never leaving Matty's.

The shots appear. We raise the glasses in a silent salute, then toss the tequila back. It burns going down, like always, and I welcome the familiarity. We slam the glasses down.

"Another." We say it at the same time.

"Hand over your keys," Anthony grouses. "I don't know what you two are up to."

Matty's lips—the lips I've kissed and fantasized about every night since—tip into a grin. "He's probably right."

I dig into my purse and slide my Jeep's key fob over to him, making sure to keep my house key. Matty pulls his truck key off the ring and slides it across the bar. Anthony takes them both and drops them into a jar behind him. Satisfied, he pours our second round.

By the third round, we've discussed our fake names, both of which are our middle names and both of which we can't believe didn't immediately give us away. By the fourth round, we're babbling about anything and everything that doesn't involve the two of us and our situation, completely ignoring the big ass elephant in the room and pretending everything is fine.

When I order a fifth round, Anthony shakes his head and holds his cell up. "I've called an Uber. Matty's buying."

"I am?" He hiccups. "I am. Of course I am. I'm a fucking gentleman."

I snicker. "Yes, you are." With a really thick dick.

He whips his head to me, eyes wide. "What did you just say?"

My own eyes go round as saucers. "What *did* I just say?"

He leans forward and whispers. At least, I hope it's a whisper. Who even knows anymore? "Did you just say I...had a thick dick?"

I lean away, my entire body heating up with a blush to end all blushes. "Um. Yes?"

His eyes widen as he breaks into a huge smile. "*Really?*"

I'm going to die.

"Uber's here. I'll walk you out." Anthony is in front of us, gesturing for us to get off the stools and follow him. "I put a twenty-five percent tip on the card, Matty. For me and the driver. You're good for it."

"Yes. Yes, I am." His chest is puffed up as he holds his hand out for mine.

I take it. "He's good for a *lot* of things, Anthony." May as well lean into it, right? If ever there was a moment to say 'fuck it' and just remove the filter, this is it.

Anthony glances at me, then at Matty, and shakes his head.

"I'm sure he is, Goldie." He opens the door and ushers us out and into the rideshare.

We're silent in the car, but we sit close, each of us using the other to prop ourselves up. Tilting my head up, I take in his shaggy hair and full lips, and when they lift in a smile, I meet his eyes. They're my undoing. They always have been.

"Goldie Dash," he murmurs, reaching his hand up to cradle my face.

Thank God I'm sitting, because the man would have just brought me to my knees.

"I'm glad it was you."

And now I'm dead, because he has killed me with the swooniest of swoony phrases.

He tilts his head, putting our lips inches apart. I remind myself to breathe. He closes the distance, and—

"We're here!" the driver announces cheerfully, prompting Matty and I to rear back and stare at each other.

"R-right," Matty says, fumbling his words and undoing his seatbelt, his cheeks blazing.

Right.

I watch Matty exit, not making my own moves to do to the same.

"Miss?"

"Mmm?"

"I've got another fare." The driver's eyes meet mine in the rearview.

Oh. *Oh.* "Of course." And then *I'm* the one blushing and getting out of the car.

I trail Matty, not sure what to do, and soon we're inside with all the animals surrounding us. "Chill out, guys," Matty says, walking to the back door off the kitchen to let the dogs out.

I pull cups out of the cabinet and fill them with water for us to chug, not remotely near sobriety. We move in sync, as though this is something we do all the time, but this has never—and I mean *never*—happened. I've been here once. Willa is the Dash sister who knows her way around here.

I shake my head. Nope. Not thinking about my sister right now. Worst idea ever. In fact, right now, in this moment, I have no sister.

Matty finishes his water, refills it, and chugs again. I might watch his Adam's apple bob with each swallow. And I might think about how sexy that is. I might also take a moment to let my eyes linger on how his shoulders fill out the T-shirt he's wearing and wonder what his chest looks like in person these days.

He lets the dogs back in, then locks the door and walks in the direction of what I can only assume is his bedroom. "Coming?"

It's midnight. I could still call an Uber and get one. Instead, I finish my water and follow. Because again: we are in 'fuck it' territory.

The room is dark, but I can see he's toeing off his shoes. I do the same. And when he flops onto the bed, face-planting into the pillow, I follow. Minus the face-in-pillow part.

When sleep comes, I welcome it with open arms.

CHAPTER 20

MATTY

I COME AWAKE in the night with a snap, immediately trying to figure out why I'm fully clothed and hugging a pillow like it's my lifeline. Within seconds, everything comes to me.

Goldie Dash is Dawn.

Holy fuck me running.

Then another realization hits me: she's next to me. Also clothed.

Shifting slowly, I roll onto my side and prop my head on my hand to look at her. For once, I let myself *really* look. I've always been so careful with her—the old 'she's my best friend's little sister' thing is absolutely a *thing*, romance novel trope or not—and it's only now, as she sleeps in my bed, that I take my time.

It's hard to believe it's her. All these years—all this *time*—and she's been right here. Not that I'm certain she wants to keep doing this.

Not that I'm certain of *anything*, in fact.

She stirs, bringing me back to the present. God, she's gorgeous. She always has been, but I've just assumed she was off-limits. I suspected she harbored a crush here and there, but figured it was just that: an innocent crush.

What wasn't innocent? The way she fucked herself with her fingers on camera. The moans she gave me while she did it. How she looked at me tonight as she told me she wanted to take me into the back and go down on her knees for me.

She breathes in, then lets out a soft whimper as she exhales. Something within me unfurls. Is this really the woman I've been looking for this whole time?

The thought is almost too much to bear.

That kiss. Christ, that *kiss*. Unable to help myself, I reach out to trace her soft lips. Lips that yielded to me so willingly the night of the masquerade ball. She knew who I was the second she saw me. Knew it was me when I kissed her. And if I'm being honest, I knew there was something about her that I recognized. That it could possibly be her. But the thought of it truly being Goldie was almost too much. And honestly, what does a guy like me have to offer a woman like her? She's sunshine incarnate, and I...I'm the welcome mat that everyone dutifully wipes their feet on. Not that I'm a pushover or anything. Just...I don't think anyone has thought about me the way *Dawn* did.

Goldie's eyes flutter open and meet mine, endlessly deep in the dark of the night. She doesn't speak, and she doesn't need to. Her eyes say everything. My fingers stay on her lips, until finally I move them, slowly, skimming down her chin and down to trace her neck, her collarbone.

I shift closer. She smells of sleep and home. Comfort. I shouldn't want this with her, but I can't make myself stop. I lean in, nuzzling into her hair, trailing my lips against her chin. All the while, my hand continues its own path, dipping into the neck of her shirt to feel the way her chest rises sharply at my touch.

She holds my gaze as I lower my mouth to hers, barely blinking. It's only when they meet that she allows her eyes to shut, and it's with a whole-body shudder.

It's impossible to deny the groan that escapes me as our lips meet. And when she sighs in return, I lose the battle completely, pulling her to me, needing to feel every part of her. Her scent, summer and sunshine, envelops me as her nails scrape against my scalp. I shiver, and she smiles against my mouth.

"You like that?"

"I do," I tell her honestly.

I get the feeling she's waiting for me to say more, but I don't know what it would be. For now, this is enough. Feeling her warm body, pliant and soft against mine, is enough.

Until she guides my hand to her hip and says, "Please."

And then I'm ruined.

Because I can't deny her. Won't. I skate my hand under the fabric of her shirt, grabbing her breast through her bra and running my thumb over her nipple. She jerks at the sensation, and now it's my turn to ask if she likes it.

"I do," she says on an exhale. "So much."

I do it again, taking her mouth with mine as she writhes on the bed beside me, and suddenly I need to be the one she's writhing against. I shift us, pulling her up to straddle me and palming her hips to thrust up against her, my cock straining against my jeans. She swivels her hips slowly, and I match her speed. She should have whatever she wants. Whatever she needs.

She braces her hands on my chest, and I move my hands beneath her shirt once more, feeling her nipples harden beneath the thin fabric of her bra as I cup her breasts. She moans. "Feels so good."

"Take what you want, Goldie," I urge, my voice low. "Use me."

"I want to feel you on top."

Done. I shift us again, putting her back on the mattress and settling between her jean-clad thighs. My cock throbs at the warmth I find there. I know if I were to put my hands down her pants, I'd find her hot and wet for me. I dip my forehead onto her neck and groan, unable to keep the image at bay. My hips find their rhythm again, pulsing slowly against hers.

"Take your shirt off," she whispers.

Reaching behind my head to yank it off, I swallow her moan as our lips meet again. I will never get enough of her lips, the tiny noises and gasps and sighs. They're my new obsession.

Her hands skate up my back, then her nails scrape down. I hiss in pleasure, thrusting harder against her and holding.

"Do that again," she commands, her voice thick.

I obey, murmuring into her ear, "I want you to come." She shivers, her hands gripping my back tight. "Think you can do that?"

She hitches a breath. "Yes."

I'm beyond desperate to take her into my mouth, but I hold off. I don't even push my hand beneath the bra, but I can feel the way her nipple hardens under my attention. "So sensitive." I nibble her bottom lip.

She swivels her hips again, harder, and I move to match her. "Don't stop," she pants. "Please. Faster."

I would never, but especially not when she asks like that. Her chin lifts as she begins to lose herself to the rising orgasm, and I bury my mouth against her neck. She smells so good.

Our movements are faster, and my own release builds. This is heaven. I brush her hair away from her face as her nails dig into my back and latch onto my jeans. Her gaze meets mine as she gasps, "Matty," then squeezes her eyes shut as the first wave hits her.

Watching—actually, no, *hearing* her come—is the best thing I've ever experienced. I follow quickly, my own release sharp and quick.

We lay there for a moment, both of us breathing hard in the aftermath, her arms wrapped tight around me, my face buried in her neck. Then I trail kisses up to her jaw, her chin, and finally her lips. Our eyes meet, and I smile gently. "Don't move."

I get up to clean the mess off me and change into sweatpants, returning as quickly as possible, getting into the bed and pulling her to me, little spoon to big spoon. When sleep overtakes me, I go willingly, the scent of summer and sunshine wrapped around me.

CHAPTER 21

GOLDIE

I WAKE UP wrapped in Matty's arms, the sound of tiny dog nails scratching on the other side of the door. A giggle escapes me.

"What's so funny?" Matty mumbles sleepily. Then, Killer whines and scratches again, and he groans. "Of course. Killer. Must be five a.m." He unfolds himself away from me and rolls out of bed, stretching and yawning.

I treat myself to the view in the dim light. He never put a shirt back on, and let's just say those cowboy fantasies have a little merit to them.

"Don't move," he says as he opens the door. Then he doubles back. "Please?"

Because of course he says please.

"I won't move," I promise. Why in the world would I want to ruin this little slice of heaven?

I hear him talking to the menagerie, and there's no stopping the smile that overtakes my face. He's so sweet with them, cooing and checking in on each one with special nicknames. Truly, he's the best.

When he returns about five minutes later, I rise onto my

knees and yank him onto the bed. He falls with an *oof*, the both of us tangling into the sheets. I go to kiss him, and he returns it, but it feels…stilted?

"What is it?" I ask, immediately sensing something is off.

He brushes the hair away from my face, his eyes searching mine. "Honestly?"

I laugh softly. "Yeah. I think we've proven that we need to be honest with each other."

His lips quirk up. "Good point."

"I'm full of them."

"What…" He exhales. "What are we doing here?"

I can feel my gaze shutter. He must notice, too, because his hand tightens on my hip.

"Goldie, come on," he pleads. "Don't shut down on me. I'm just…not confused. That's not the word. But I have no idea what we're doing."

I should have a bit more mercy on him, I suppose. He's still coming to terms with the fact it's me. "Do you want to keep this quiet?"

"No," he says immediately. "I'm not—that's not it at all. I don't want to *hide* you."

"But you also aren't sure what we're doing?"

He nods. "Should we…go on a date?"

Part of me wants to start a cheer, complete with tumbles megaphones. The other part realizes he's not yet convinced. "Where?"

He hums. "Why don't we grab Mexican? People will think it's just friends getting dinner."

"But we *never* get dinner together."

"Sure. But that doesn't mean we *can't*."

"Okay," I agree. I lean forward to kiss him, and he's a little more relaxed this time. "It's obvious we've got chemistry, right? Now we just need to figure out if we really like each other like this."

The relief that washes over his face is obvious, even in the dim morning light.

Spoiler alert: I already know I like him. But it's clear he needs a bit more time to sort this out.

"So, a date that's not a date at the Mexican restaurant? We keep this under the radar while we figure it all out."

He nods again, his smile genuine. I can practically feel the nerves seep out of his skin.

I scoot closer, unable to keep my hands to myself anymore. "Does that mean we can make out some more?" I grin cheekily, running a hand up his arm and to his chest.

God, his chest. It's what my dreams are made of.

"Yeah." He smiles. "We can do that."

I reach for him, relishing the solid weight of him as we sink into the mattress. His kisses set me on fire, and the way our bodies fit together is insane. He seems to know exactly what I want and when, taking my mouth in a deep kiss before pulling back to linger on my lips.

We stare at each other. I don't know what he's thinking, but I know that I could welcome the dawn every morning with him for the rest of my life and be content. I'd be *more* than content. It'd be a dream come true. Looking into his deep brown eyes and swimming in the kindness I see there forever? Sign me up.

A bit later, we get up and Matty makes a pot of coffee. I toast some bread and we have a simple breakfast surrounded by Killer, Kitty, Crush, the orange tabby, and Spot, the calico cat. Apparently Hedgie prefers to sleep in, so I don't get to see him.

Matty calls an Uber for us to take back to the bar. The second we climb into the back seat, I feel him withdraw. It's visceral, the disappointment that floods me. Is this how he's going to be in public? Even though he said he *didn't* want to keep this quiet?

I fold my hands in my lap and squeeze. I can't spiral. I'm better than this.

At least, I'd like to think I am. There's a difference between what I think and the way I actually react, though, isn't there? I guess my true colors are about to come flying out. Maybe I'm *not* all sunshine and rainbows. Only time will tell.

We arrive at the bar, neither of us having spoken the whole ride. I'm sure the driver must think this is a morning-after gone terribly wrong, and he might be right. The idea sours my stomach.

We get out and the driver leaves, and we face each other.

Matty grins. "How did I miss this thing when I came here last night?" He nods at my Jeep, decked out with its row of rubber ducks gracing the dashboard.

"Probably because you beat me here," I tease.

He huffs out a wry laugh. "That's right."

"Well…" I trail off, suddenly unsure and hating myself for it. "I guess…I'll see you later?"

"Yeah." He nods and shoves his hands in his pockets.

I eye him. "Right."

"Okay."

"Um…okay. Call me? I mean, call me." I make myself sound decisive. *What is* wrong *with me?*

"Will do."

I should kiss him. He isn't leaving. We literally dry humped last night, and he isn't making a move to kiss me. But he's also not turning to leave. So…what now?

"Okay!" I force a smile and a laugh, and go up on my toes to peck him on the cheek.

It's awkward as hell. He pats my side stiffly, and I back away as quick as I can.

"Talk to you later," I manage, then turn to get in my Jeep. It must be the signal he needs, because he makes his way across the empty lot to his truck.

I pull my phone out and pretend it's the most interesting thing I've ever seen, desperate for him to leave. Finally, he exits the lot. I lower my head to the steering wheel and bang it.

Despite the hellscape that was our goodbye scene back there, I've just gotten everything I ever wanted. Right? Basically, I think I have?

But if that's true, then can someone please explain to me why I thought it was a good idea to suggest we basically be each other's dirty little secret?

CHAPTER 22

MATTY

I PULL TO a stop sign, and once I make sure no one is behind me, I bang my head against the steering wheel.

What the actual fuckety fuck am I *doing*?

Do I like her? Is doing this in secret a good idea, or is it the absolute worst idea in the history of worst ideas?

Probably the latter.

A honk sounds behind me, and I straighten and keep driving, waving my hand in apology to the extremely irate old lady who is now—what the *hell?*—speeding past me and flipping me the bird?

Really?

That's what we're doing this morning?

I'm too stunned to do anything but laugh, and ooh, boy, this woman is displeased. Her frown deepens and she waves her middle finger to and fro, hitting the gas and whipping in front of me.

Guess I'm the asshole this morning in more ways than one.

I swing back to my house to grab Killer before heading to the clinic, spiraling all the way. Even Killer's sweet little face licks can't pull me out of my worries.

I need to figure out if I really like Goldie the way I liked Dawn.

But she *is* Dawn.

The whole thing is still a bit of a mind-fuck. And I can't get last night out of my head. The way we came together, wrapping around each other in the safety of the dark. The way we *actually* came together.

I can't believe I've had video sex with my best friend's little sister.

I can't believe I came last night with my best friend's little sister.

Jesus. I really am a walking romance novel right now.

The problem is, I'm not sure I've got a happily ever after waiting for me. What if we try this, and we flame out? I'm super boring, and Goldie is the exact opposite. She'll tire of me eventually. Probably *faster* than eventually. What happens to my relationship with Willa? Sure, she's got Reid now, and that's been an adjustment, but Willa—hell, her entire family—they've been such an integral part of my life. What if I lose that? Because it's not like my own mom and dad are over there waving and yelling for me to come over and get cozy. They left this town the second I graduated high school, fleeing like they'd robbed a damn bank. And the years leading up to their departure weren't that cuddly to begin with.

As if on cue, Willa texts and invites me to dinner with her and Reid that night.

I drop Killer off with Liv and watch him sniff around, then curl into his cushy kingdom behind the reception desk. Honestly, that dog has a better life that me. I can guarantee that I would *not* get the kind of love and attention he does if my head was shaped like an apple, I shook almost constantly, and my cream-colored hair was almost see-through.

REID KNOWS SOMETHING IS UP WHEN I ARRIVE AT
their house that night. The second Willa leaves the kitchen to go to
the restroom, he pulls his Investigator Reid hat on and turns on me.

"What is going on with you, man? Is it Dawn?"

I flinch, and Reid sees it.

His eyes narrow. "Talk to me. What's going on? We've not
caught up since the masquerade thing. Did she like Cowboy
Matty?"

I swallow. *Boy, did she ever.* "Yeah. It was, ah, it was great."

Reid lifts a single eyebrow. "It was *great*? The hell does that
mean, *great*?"

"It means it was great! She's great."

"So what's happening now? Have you seen each other since?"

"S-sort of," I stammer.

"Explain."

"I…"

I'm saved by Willa coming back. She takes one look and
gestures between us. "Um, what's going on here? And don't
say—"

"Nothing," Reid and I answer simultaneously.

She crosses her arms. "Guys."

Reid laughs. "Seriously, it's nothing. Don't worry about it."

"I don't believe either of you. It better not be something about
my birthday. You know I don't like surprises."

"I would *never* let a birthday surprise happen to you," I promise. "You know that. Besides, your birthday is forever away."

She twists her lips and studies me. "It's about the girl, isn't it?
You better not have told him more than you told me, Matthew
James Brodigan."

"Whoa, whoa, whoa," Reid steps into her line of sight, and I
swear I nearly fall to my knees to kiss the man's feet right then. I
don't know if he's been subjected to Willa's particular brand of
questioning, but it involves an impressive layer cake of guilt,

threats, jokes, and things that seemingly have nothing to do with anything, until suddenly, *bam*. She's got you.

And I cannot be subjected to her tonight.

She harrumphs. "You're lucky I like both of you. *And* that I'm not cooking. Because otherwise, I'd stop cooking and you two would be left to fend for yourselves."

I smile. "You know, ever since Reid got here, I don't think that threat is nearly as effective as it used to be."

She sticks her tongue out at me. "Whatever. Come on, let's go hang out in the living room while my sweet boyfriend cooks us all dinner."

"With pleasure." I hold my arm out for her to take, then look back at Reid as we leave the kitchen. *"Thank you,"* I mouth.

"You owe me," he mouths back.

My stomach clenches at the thought. This *is* the guy who was undercover with a drug cartel for two years, after all. I have a bad feeling he's got some seriously creative ways to get stories out of me.

But I hold strong all night long. I stick to my guns when he glares at me when Willa's back is turned, and I hold firm when she starts to doze on the couch and Reid walks with Killer and me to my car.

"You're keeping something from me," he pouts. "Why won't you tell me?"

I sigh. "Would you believe me if I said it was for your own good?"

"Probably not."

"Too bad, because guess what? It's for your own good."

"I don't think I like you very much right now," he huffs as I start the truck.

I roll the window down and hold my hands out for Killer. "Hand over the chihuahua."

He cradles the tiny dog against his chest, then gives him a

smooch on his head. "Cute little thing. I should keep him until you start telling me what's going on."

I consider him. "You would, wouldn't you?"

He hands Killer over. "I would."

By the time I get home and feed the dogs, the cats, and Hedgie, I'm no clearer on what to do than I was at the beginning of the day. I need someone to talk to, and normally it'd be Willa.

Clearly, there's the tiny matter of a conflict of interest happening there.

Goldie hasn't sent me any messages today. Maybe she's just as messed up about all this as me.

When I finally get to bed, all I smell is Goldie.

What would James do?

Sighing, I sit up in bed and pull up the *Blinding Love* app.

> Good night,

I don't send it. Good night...*what?* Good night, Dawn? Good night, exclamation point? Good night with an emoji? "Send *something*, asshole," I mutter. Finally, I delete the comma, add a period, and send the damn text.

JAMES

> Good night.

Her reply comes moments later.

DAWN

> Sweet dreams 🖤

Satisfied I've not completely fucked this up, I blacken the screen and roll over. When I finally fall asleep, I dream about Goldie.

CHAPTER 23

GOLDIE

WAKING UP BY myself is bullshit.

I'm mad the second I open my eyes. Mad that all it took was one night of sleeping in the same bed as Matty to ruin me for, well, *ever*. That asshole.

I roll over and grab my phone, hoping he's reached out in the time I've slept. But other than the good night texts we exchanged, he hasn't. I figured it was better to let him work his way through the whole "holy crap, it's my best friend's little sister" thing, if I had to guess.

It still stings, though.

And hell if I'm going to sit around and moon over it. That's not how I operate.

But first: coffee.

Once I'm up and showered, fresh cup of coffee in hand, I pull up our thread in the app. I scroll all the way to the top, then skim it through. Reading it now, it's obvious we've been falling for each other the whole time. I know he's into me. That's not the issue. The issue is his lack of bravery.

Ooh, damn. I went there, didn't I?

But something tells me that he won't react well if I just text him and tell him to quit being a scaredy-cat. I start a new message in the app.

JAMES*(DAWN)*

> I should tell you something.

A few minutes later, he answers.

JAMES

> What's that?

> My name isn't really Dawn.

> You don't say?

> It's Goldie. Goldie Dash.

> Nice to meet you, Goldie Dash. I'm Matty Brodigan. But I guess you know that.

I smile and type back.

> I do. So…

> So. ☺

I take a deep breath and decide to dive right in.

> Here's the thing. I liked you when I thought you were James. And…

I hit send, needing to gather my thoughts on how exactly to say this.

JAMES

> Jeez, Goldie. Way to keep a guy hanging

> I'm trying to figure out how to say this in a way that isn't weird

> Isn't this already weird?

I don't know. Is it?

Well, now that you ask…

See? You don't know either.

Okay, you win. I'll wait patiently. But you should
know that Killer isn't nearly as patient as me.

A picture comes through, and it's Killer, mid-bark, looking far
more adorable than any little dog has a right to. The *aww* that
leaves me is high-pitched, and I laugh to myself.

DAWN

I love that dog

Same.

Okay. Here goes. You ready?

I'm ready. Killer is here to comfort me if I need it.

Good.

Shoot.

I'm trying. You keep interrupting me.

This is me being patient, Goldie.

UGH, Matty!

Okay. Here goes.

I take a deep breath and type.

> I like you even more, now that I know it's you. I'm guessing you've always known I crushed on you a little, right? But it was always just a little crush. Nothing crazy. I figured you'd never look at me as anything other than Willa's sister. But now that whatever this is has happened, I think you're freaked out. And I don't want you to be. But I don't know how to make you *not* freak out.

I hit send and groan. I needed to send that, but crap, that was kind of the pits.

Bubbles appear at the bottom of my screen. I jiggle my legs and sip at my coffee. *Now* who's the impatient one?

JAMES

> You're right. I'm freaking out. I don't know what to do.

> What is it about us that's so appalling?

> It's not appalling—not at all.

> Because we're not the first people this has happened to.

> I know.

> Then what is it?

> I...crap, Goldie, I don't know. I need to process all this. Can you give me that?

His answer is a gut punch. But I nod stiffly to myself and answer him.

> Didn't seem like you needed much processing last night.

> You can't tell, but I just flinched over here.

I don't respond. What am I supposed to say? I'm not going to comfort him. He's a big boy. A moment later, his message appears.

JAMES

You're right. I'm the asshole here. I know enough to know that. But I also know that I have no fucking clue how I feel right now.

Sighing, I type back.

DAWN

I'm not going to say "it's okay," but I'm also not going to be mad.

Thank you.

I click my phone off and toss it onto the couch with a thud, then slide down until I'm half off the thing. I'm better than this. I don't need to be all up in my feels just because a boy isn't sure if he likes me.

But I am.

And it pisses me off. The whole thing pisses me off. I groan loudly. What am I going to do?

Then I sit up. I need to get to work. Today, I'm heading out to Black Stables, a black-owned horse farm a couple of hours north, to do a profile. Not many people know the history of black-owned stables, and I want to change that.

I jump up and get ready, throwing on jeans and comfortable work boots—which most people wouldn't believe I actually own, but a girl's gotta be prepared for anything—and finish the outfit with a soft T-shirt and light flannel button-down. I grab my notebook and camera bag and take off.

Two hours later, I'm pulling through gates proudly proclaiming WELCOME TO BLACK STABLES, the letters in bright white against the black metal surrounding them. I pull up to a small house, my Jeep's tires crunching on the gravel drive. A tall, perilously thin older man steps onto the porch, tipping his worn cowboy hat at me in greeting.

I get out and he lopes down the steps, extending his hand in greeting. "Miss Dash." He grins, his dark skin crinkling beneath the brim of his hat. "I'm Jack Black—not the actor. Nice to meet you."

I laugh and shake his hand. "Pretty sure you were named that first, right?"

He nods, his smile broadening. "You catch on fast."

"Thanks so much for letting me visit," I say as I pull out my camera. "I remember going to Birmingham for a Veterans Day parade when I was a kid and seeing horses from your stable in the parade. Blew my mind."

He chuckles. "The horses, or the black men and women on them?"

"The horses," I say honestly. "They were *huge* to me! Plus, they were spinning and going up on their hind legs, and the riders were all kitted out in sparkles and fancy fringe. I was dazzled."

"Tell the truth, now." He slides a teasing glance at me. "Did you want to be a cowgirl after that?"

"Heck yeah, I did," I laugh. "Sadly, there are precious few opportunities to be a cowgirl when you live in a small beach town. But I'm thrilled to be here today."

"We're happy to have you," he responds, then tips his head toward the stables in the distance. "Ready to get started?"

Jack takes me to a bright red barn situated on a hill, the sky a flawless blue behind it. I snap some pictures as we go, already settling into the visit and tossing questions at him.

When we enter the building, I'm surrounded by the smells. Horse, hay, leather, and the always-present manure, despite an incredibly clean barn. I hear the soft snicker of horses beneath the raucous shouts of folks mucking out the stalls and grooming horses.

Jack waves me farther in. "Welcome to a horse stable, Miss Dash."

"Call me Goldie, please."

An hour passes, and then another, and soon it's lunchtime. I join a huge group of people at a set of picnic tables behind the house, and we dig in to a simple meal of build-your-own sand-wiches, fruit, chips, and chocolate chip cookies. With sweet tea and lemonade, obviously.

After lunch, Jack declares it's time to get me on a horse, and I'm practically vibrating with excitement.

As we approach a different stable than the one we'd been at this morning, he looks over at me. "You been on a horse before, Goldie?"

"Does riding a pony at the fair count?"

He laughs. "It does not. Follow me. I've got the perfect horse for you." He leads me into the building and to one of the farthest stalls. He waves me forward, and I gasp with pleasure. "This is Sweetie Pie. She's as good as her name."

Sweetie Pie clops forward a few steps and dips her dappled gray head out of the stall, sniffing at Jack's pockets for the peppermints I've learned he keeps there. He produces one and she takes it, snorting softly.

Jack steps back and I take his place, reaching my hand up to pet Sweetie Pie's velvety nose. She blinks at me and pushes her nose under my hand, an invitation to pet more. I do. "Aren't you a sweetie?" I coo at her.

"Exactly," Jack chuckles.

He gets her out of the stall and walks me through tacking her up. His horse is Biggie, a sleek black stallion with white on his hooves and a haughty attitude. Biggie is all ready to go, so we walk them outside. Jack puts a stool next to Sweetie Pie, then helps me up.

"Whoa," I breathe. Sweetie Pie shifts beneath me, and I stroke her neck. "You gonna be good for me?"

Jack mounts Biggie in one swift movement, settling in the saddle and looking over at me. "Grab onto the reins and hold onto her with your thighs a bit. Nothing too crazy, but you can't just hang there. Sweetie Pie will follow Biggie, so just hold onto her reins and don't fall off."

I laugh. "You make it sound so simple."

He grins. "It is."

We make our way over a hill and onto a well-worn trail through the woods that border the farm. It's incredibly peaceful, the steady sound of the horses' hooves against the packed dirt, the sound of birds calling to each other, the slight breeze rustling the late spring leaves. I take a deep breath and let it out, taking the moment to empty my mind and center myself. The last few weeks have been…a *lot*…and I'm grateful for the silence that Jack's given me. Riding a horse, it turns out, is incredibly therapeutic.

By the time we emerge from the trail and back into the sunlight, I'm more settled and content than I've been in weeks.

Which is good, because there, before my very eyes, is Cowboy Matty.

I blink. This is a mirage, right?

Matty is on a brown and white horse in the center of a paddock just to our right, wearing the very same black cowboy hat he had on at the masquerade ball, along with a thin white tee, faded jeans, and the cowboy boots I rarely see him without.

I blink again, then startle as Jack calls out, "Hey, Doc!"

Matty tips his hat, then smirks at me.

Smirks.

Then I realize my jaw has unhinged itself and is practically on Sweetie Pie's head, so I snap it shut and try to get it together.

Because Cowboy Matty is freaking *hot*. He kicks the horse into a trot, and that asshole sits in the saddle like he's done it for years, holding the reins like a natural and leaning down to whisper in the horse's ear. When he straightens, the horse goes into some kind of complicated dance, reminding me of the long-ago Veterans Day parade in Birmingham that I'd mentioned to Jack.

I finally find my voice. "How do you know Ma—I mean, Dr. Brodigan?"

"He's our vet," Jack answers. "Great kid. Figured you'd know him. He's from your town, isn't he?"

I nod, unable to keep my eyes off Matty. "How does he know how to do that?"

"Doc ain't doing anything. That's all Chuck D. He's a prancer through and through; loves to show off."

Someone is showing off, all right, but I don't think it's the horse.

And I am not mad about it.

Matty's biceps flex, and the sun literally glints off them. *This is ridiculous.* I've felt those arms around me. I've had those lips on mine. And those hips moving back and forth in the saddle? Yeah, they've done that between my legs.

I barely suppress a whimper.

"Chuck D. was limping, so we called Doc in. Seems he's doing a lot better." He leads us to the paddock, nodding at the cowboy leaning against the fence in acknowledgment.

Matty trots Chuck D. toward us, grinning like the Cheshire Cat. He knows *exactly* what he's doing. "Hey, Jack. Goldie."

"Doc," Jack says. "How's my main guy?"

"He's gonna be fine. Pulled a muscle in his foreleg, nothing a little rest won't fix. I've left you some topical salve; I think that's all he needs."

Jack nods. "Join us the rest of the way?"

"Be happy to."

The three of us make our slow way back to the stable. Jack dismounts and helps me down, then leads both horses away without so much as a backward glance. Matty's horse is also led into the stable by another person, leaving the two of us alone.

For a moment, neither of us speaks.

"Working on a story?" Matty asks, glancing at my camera bag and back.

I nod. "Been here all morning. I didn't know you'd be here."

He shrugs and smiles sheepishly. "I did. Know that you'd be here, that is." I must make a face, because he holds his hands up, even as a blush makes its way up his cheeks. "I'm not stalking you, I swear. When they called me this morning, they told me Jack would be busy with a reporter from Lucky. I knew there was only one reporter from Lucky who'd make the trek up here. And when I got here, I saw you and Jack, and then later I saw you at lunch with everyone."

I tilt my head. "And you didn't want to say hello either of those times?" I don't get it.

"No way. You were working. And…" He looks down and kicks the dirt.

I laugh. "It's hard work coming up with words, isn't it, cowboy?"

He grins sheepishly. "Hey, I never said I was a cowboy. *You* did."

I raise an eyebrow. "Looked just like a cowboy on that stallion a few minutes ago."

He blushes more. "That was silly of me. I shouldn't have—"

"Looked like a damn snack up there, like you were born for a life on the farm? No, you shouldn't have," I tease. "But come on, out with it. What's got you tongue-tied?"

He adjusts the cowboy hat, and I know it's unintentional on his part, but *damn*, even that move is stupidly sexy. Maybe I need to read some cowboy romance. He clears his throat and meets my eyes. "I've never seen you like this. Working. You're different. Like, you're Goldie, but you're also so…*not* Goldie."

I narrow my eyes. "I'm not sure if I should take that as a compliment or an insult."

He smiles. "It's a compliment, I promise." After a beat, he says, "Let me take you on a date."

"Me? Or Dawn?" I probably shouldn't push him, but I can't help it.

"You, Goldie. Just you. Tomorrow night."

"Really?"

He meets my eyes. "Really."

I don't hesitate. "Yes."

CHAPTER 24

MATTY

I PULL UP in front of Agatha's house and hop out of my truck, only to be stopped by the suspiciously happy woman herself.

"Matty! Hello!" She waves and sing-songs my name.

I throw a hand up in greeting, but don't veer in the direction of her porch. "Hi, Agatha."

Sensing my plan to slip by without a conversation, Agatha hustles down her porch steps and aims toward me. *Damn. Guess we're talking.* "How are things with our girl?"

I raise an eyebrow. "Willa? She's...good?" I'm not sure how to answer.

She swats my arm gently. "Oh, you're funny. Not Willa, silly. Goldie. How are things with *Goldie?*"

I blink. How the hell—you know what? Doesn't matter. "Things are...fine," I answer. I'm not loving the way I keep hesitating to answer her questions about the Dash sisters, but this whole line of questioning has me way out of my depth.

Agatha's eyes brighten. "That's so good to hear! You know, when she was messaging you on that app, I thought it was the most amazing thing. The two of you—who would have thought

I'd be responsible for *both* those girls' happiness?" She holds a hand over her heart and gazes into the distance. "Truly wonderful. A gift, really."

I have no idea what she's going on about, but I also know that I need to wrap this up. Immediately, if not sooner. "A gift," I echo.

She beams, which tells me I've probably said something really stupid.

Wouldn't be the first time.

I hitch a thumb toward the carriage house. "I've got to, you know, go."

She clasps her hands to her chest. "Of course you do." She leans forward and winks. "Be good, now."

If I didn't know any better, I'd swear she was talking about… well.

"But I'm sure you are," she says as she turns.

My jaw drops open. Holy shit. She really *was* talking about sex.

Shaking my head, I close the short distance to Goldie's door and rap on the window.

"Come in!" she calls. "Door's unlocked!"

I open the door and cross the threshold. I've not been in the place since Willa lived here, and a lot is the same. As I move through the kitchen and into the living room, though, one thing is noticeably absent. "Where are the doilies?"

Goldie snorts from the bathroom. "Packed away like the menaces they are." She emerges with a bright smile, and I'm shocked into silence again.

She's gorgeous.

Absolutely, drop-dead, I-have-been-an-absolute-fool-all-these-years flawless.

Seeing my obvious glitch—which, come to think of it, seems to be a pattern of mine when faced with Goldie lately—she twirls. When her bright blue eyes meet mine again, she asks, "You like?"

"I like," I croak. Then I clear my throat. "You're wearing that to Mexican?"

She laughs. "Matty, I've worn this around you before. Literally. This exact same outfit."

"Well, that settles it."

She furrows her brow slightly. "Settles what?"

"That I'm an absolute idiot," I declare. "Because you look amazing." I close the distance to her, unable to take it anymore, and pull her to me. She's in tight, dark denim that flares over platform sandals and a simple yellow tank top, with a flowy sheer yellow shirt on top. I have no idea what to call it, but she embodies effortless beauty. How in the ever-loving hell have I missed her all these years?

Again: an absolute idiot. Me. Very stupid.

She drapes her arms over my shoulders as I run my palms down her sides to rest on her hips, then smirks. "You gonna kiss me, Matty, or just look at me like you're gobsmacked?"

"Can I do both?"

She threads her fingers through the hair at the nape of my neck. "Kiss me, you fool."

Gladly. I close the distance and thank whatever heavenly creature was clearly looking over me all these years. Because if I've got the chance to make Goldie mine? I need to take it.

In the truck, I keep my hand on her thigh, needing to touch her no matter how insignificant the contact. And in the restaurant, it takes everything I have to sit directly across from her instead of sliding next to her in the booth.

We each order a beer, but when the server walks away to get them, I fix Goldie with a stare. "I'm only having one drink," I tell her.

She nods, a soft smile on her lips. "Yeah?"

"I don't want to fall asleep like last time."

Her eyes twinkle. "You sound awfully confident something's going to happen."

I lean forward. "See, that's where you're wrong."

The server returns with our beers, and we order our food: street tacos for Goldie and enchiladas verdes for me. When he leaves, Goldie arches a brow as she pops a chip in her mouth. "How exactly am I wrong?"

I grab a chip and dunk it in the salsa. "I didn't say anything was going to happen. But you just did."

She grins. "I most definitely did not."

"You insinuated it."

"*You* insinuated it, not me!" Her smile widens.

I shrug. "Guess we'll just have to see."

She shakes her head. "I like you like this, you know," she says, her voice softening.

"Like what?"

"Like…like you're James. Except you're Matty." She breaks eye contact. "I don't know if that makes sense."

"It does. And for the record," I take another chip and swim it through the salsa, "it's taking everything I have not to reach over and hold your hand right now."

Bright spots of color appear on her cheeks. "Really?"

"Yes, really." Then I lower my voice. "I liked it better at Hall's, where at least we knew Anthony didn't give a damn about what was going on."

She smiles in agreement. "He's something, isn't he?"

"If by 'something' you mean speaks in grunts and short sentences and is so different from Ox and Levi that it's hard to believe they all came from the same parents, then yes, he's something."

Laughing, she agrees. "That's *exactly* what I mean."

When Carmen comes by after our meal to see if we'd like a round of shots, we decline. "You sure? Last time you were here…" She trails off and smirks.

Yeah, last time I was here was my birthday, when I was beyond drunk.

"I'm sure," I say. Carmen leaves and I meet Goldie's gaze. "You know, that's the night I created my profile."

Her eyes flare. "Your birthday?"

I nod. "I kept looking at Willa and Reid and thinking how much I wanted what they have." An embarrassed snicker comes out of me. "Sorry. I shouldn't—"

"I'm glad you did," Goldie interrupts me. She looks around furtively, then reaches her hand out to touch my knuckles. "I can't imagine this past month without…" She clears her throat. "Without you."

My heart swells. *This could really be happening.* "Yeah?"

Her expression is soft. "Yeah."

I grab the check and stand. "C'mon. Let's get out of here."

She rises. "Your place or mine?"

"Is mine okay? The dogs…"

"Of course," she agrees.

I pay and we leave, and this time, her hand rests in mine all the way home. I'd like to say I don't think about how well our hands fit together, but I do.

Inside, I let the dogs out and Goldie wanders over to Hedgie's tank, cooing over him as though he's the cutest thing she's ever seen.

"Wanna let him out?"

She looks over at me, her face pure delight, but it's gone a second later. "Not right now."

I cross the room. "Something wrong?"

Her cheeks redden again and she looks down. "It's just…"

I hook my fingers through her belt loops and pull her to me, inhaling her summery scent. "Just what?" I murmur, leaning down to kiss her.

She sighs against my lips. "This is why."

I pepper her chin with kisses as I make my way to her ear, kissing the skin just below it. "Why what?" I prompt.

Killer barks and scratches on the door. Goldie giggles.

"Because I'm not interested in playing with a hedgehog when I can play with you."

My dick agrees with that, twitching as I continue kissing her neck. "Fair," I mutter.

Killer yips again.

"You gonna let him in?" Goldie asks, amused.

I groan. "Hold that thought." When I return to the living room, Killer and Kitty hot on my heels, Goldie pulls off the sheer top she'd had on over the tank, revealing a sliver of skin above her jeans. My mouth dries.

She drops the shirt onto the couch with a smile. "I like that look."

I take a step toward her. "And what's that?"

"Like you want to devour me." Her voice is breathy.

"Because I do."

Her eyes darken as she licks her lips. "Good."

I move, eating the distance in two steps and cupping her head to bring her mouth to mine.

She tips onto her toes, thrusting her tongue into my mouth and matching my intensity. I walk her backward, guiding her to my bedroom and away from the animals. She doesn't hesitate, trusting me to move her where she needs to go.

When we get to my room, I kick the door shut, sealing us in darkness.

"Wait," she says, coming up for air.

I stop everything, putting my hands up and releasing her.

"Light. I want light."

I smirk. "We've done pretty well in the dark, don't you think?"

She laughs quietly. "I want to see you, Matty."

And even though the words are brave, her vulnerability is clear. I understand immediately, and move to turn on the bedside lamp. The room is thrown into a soft light, and Goldie's shoulders drop.

"Good?"

She nods. "Good."

This time, it's her who closes the distance, her knees knocking against my legs as she meets me beside the bed. "Are you nervous?" I ask.

She bites her lip. "I shouldn't be."

"Doesn't mean you can't be." A beat passes, then I admit, "*I'm* nervous."

Her eyes fly to mine. "What do you have to be nervous for?"

"Are you kidding?" I run my fingers down her cheek, to her chin, then down to the neckline of her tank top. I trace it, watching the goosebumps form in my wake. "I've got the most beautiful woman in the world in my bedroom, and it's been...a long time since I've been with anyone. It's entirely possible I'm going to mess this up."

"I've seen your dick, Matty," Goldie assures me. "There is absolutely no way you can fuck this up."

I throw my head back and laugh. Then I nearly swallow my tongue because when I look at her again, she's pulled her tank top off.

And she's wearing a yellow fucking bra.

CHAPTER 25

GOLDIE

MATTY BLINKS AT me, dazed once again. My heart is beating so hard that I have to look down to make sure it's not erupting from the skin. But nope, still tucked safely away. Meanwhile, Matty's gone stone-still in front of me.

Clearly, I need to take control.

I lift my hands to his shirt, taking the button between my fingers and undoing it.

He inhales.

I meet his eyes. "Are you okay?"

He swallows. "I think so."

"Do we need to stop?" *Please say no, please say no.*

"No."

Thank God.

His eyes drop to my bra. "It's...yellow."

I undo another button. "It is."

He lifts a hand as though he's going to touch me, then lets it drop.

I pop another button out. Then another. "This is much better than the video, you know," I say softly.

"Definitely," he rasps.

"I knew it was you," I confess.

"I know."

"And seeing you unbutton your shirt through that screen?" I lick my lips and meet his eyes. "It nearly melted my brain." I undo the last button. "Then I saw your dick, and I almost passed out."

He laughs softly, his hands hanging by his side. "And now?"

"Now…" I push the shirt off his shoulders and let my hands rest against his tan, strong chest, feeling the heat seep into my palms as he inhales. "This is perfect." I press my lips to his sternum, breathing him in. His familiar scent, a simple mix of soap, deodorant, and laundry detergent, is home. He is everything I have ever wanted, created just for me and wrapped up in the most perfect package imaginable.

Matty brings a hand up to brush my hair back from my neck, and I shiver. "Tell me what you want, Golden."

I meet his eyes. "What did you—"

"You're the perfect one, Goldie." He smiles affectionately. "You're golden. You always have been."

The nickname unleashes something feral in me, removing whatever restraints I had and tossing them to the floor. I bring my mouth back to his chest and nip at the skin. He hisses as our eyes meet. "Don't treat me like I'm fragile, Matty. That's all I ask."

He squeezes my ass hard in response, then brings his hands to the front of my jeans, undoing them while his lips trail hot kisses down the center of my chest, skipping over the bra and moving to my stomach as he goes onto his knees. Tucking his hands into the band of my jeans, he pulls them down and off over the strappy sandals. As he runs his hands over the sandals and my feet, he looks up at me, his dark brown eyes blown with lust and wonder. "They're yellow."

"You saw them all night. You know they're yellow."

He trails his fingers along my ankles, and when he speaks, his voice is low. "They're staying on."

I hitch a breath, standing before him in bra, panties and heels. "Okay."

Still on his knees before me, he brings his nose to my belly and inhales as I thread my nails through his hair, doing it hard like I know he wants. When his hands grip the sides of my sheer yellow panties, he shudders, then growls as he exhales. His tongue darts out and licks down the sheer fabric. Then he scrapes his teeth down, and I jolt at the heat it shoots through me.

"Matty."

"Sit on the bed and spread your legs."

I obey, sitting and widening my knees as far as they can go, then arching my back and using my palms to push them a little farther when I see the way his eyes darken and his jaw slackens. *I'm* doing this to him. *Me.*

"You're already wet for me." It's a statement.

"Of course," I whisper.

He meets my eyes. "Move them."

I hook a finger through the thin fabric and pull the panties to one side, revealing my bare pussy for his perusal.

His eyes nearly roll back in his head as he takes me in. "Fucking flawless." One hand comes to rest on my breast, the other traces the inside of my thigh. I can barely breathe when his eyes meet mine as his mouth locks over my nipple and sucks it through the thin fabric of my bra.

"Fuck, Matty." My pulse is racing.

He moans, his hand squeezing my breast as he sucks the other. I arch into his mouth and pull him closer, needing more. Needing him inside me.

As if reading my thoughts, he moves his free hand up my leg and pushes a finger into me. We groan together. "God, you feel good."

"Yes, you do," I answer. He unsnaps my bra, and I slide it off, our lips meeting in a series of frantic kisses as I wrap my arms around him, needing every bit of connection I can get.

He pushes a second finger into me, curling them both at the exact right angle. My hips jerk, and I whimper against his lips, the sweetest of aches beginning to swirl. "Matthew—"

He growls, his fingers going even deeper. I moan his name again, my voice dropping an octave as he bends to take a nipple into his mouth. Without the bra in the way, his tongue lights me on fire.

"Oh God," I gasp.

"Come for me, Golden."

The name shouldn't spear into me the way it does, hitting my heart with an accuracy that tips me into territory I'm not ready to think about. But it also sends me into overdrive, and when his thumb presses on my clit, I detonate, yelling his name as I climax. My whole body trembles as wave after wave takes me, my nails digging into his back while I hold him to me with the other.

He works me through the orgasm, slowing his mouth and fingers as I relax. With a final lick of my nipple, Matty straightens and pulls his fingers out, looking me dead in the eye as he licks them.

"Fuck, that's hot," I exhale, not letting myself look away from his dark brown eyes.

He grins, then rises. I stop his hands as they go to unbutton his jeans, swatting them away and doing it myself. "My turn."

He shakes his head. "No."

I ignore the protest and shove his jeans down, smirking up at him with doe eyes. "Don't really see you stopping me."

In response, he backs out of my grip and pulls his jeans the rest of the way off, standing before me in tented black boxer briefs.

I lick my lips at the sight. "I can't wait to get my mouth on you."

His expression is dark and sexy. "My house, my rules. And tonight is all about you."

I partly want to pout, but at the same time, when has a guy ever affirmatively chosen my pleasure over his own?

Never. The answer is never.

Matty smirks, satisfied. "That's what I thought. Take off your panties."

I look down at my heels. "The shoes?"

"On."

I slide my panties off and stay on the edge of the mattress as he removes his boxer briefs. My eyes flare as I take all of him in. He's trim, not bulky, his muscles compact and not overly defined. I want to lick every part of him: his neck, his smooth chest, taut stomach, the lines above his hips, and his perfect thighs, rippling as he nears me once more.

"On the bed, Goldie."

I obey, and his eyes darken as they land on my shoes. He keeps his gaze on me as he pulls a condom out of his bedside table and tosses it onto the mattress, and then he's lowering himself to me, his cock heavy between my thighs as he settles between them and takes my mouth in another kiss. I bend my knee as his hand glides up my thigh and down my calf, and he groans into my mouth as his fingers caress my foot and the straps around it.

"So fucking sexy."

I grip his thick shaft, smiling as he grunts in surprised pleasure. "I've wanted my hands on this for a while, you know. I have to cop a feel."

He laughs and adjusts himself to give me more access. "Fine, but your mouth stays up here tonight." And with that, he slants his lips over mine, claiming me in a bruising kiss that promises only pleasure.

Our hands are everywhere, touching, caressing, squeezing,

and it's not long before I'm squirming to have him inside me. "Matty," I start.

But he already knows, because he reaches over for the condom and goes onto his knees. He rips the foil and rolls it on, then positions himself above me, the blunt tip of his cock nudging my entrance as his gaze takes us in.

Wordlessly, I pull him to me. And as our mouths meet, he enters, stretching me deliciously. He pulls out and pushes again, going a bit farther. The third time, he fills me deeper and wider than I've ever felt.

"Hang on," he grits, his whole body still as we both adjust.

"Guess that video wasn't lying," I giggle.

He huffs out a laugh and drops his head into my neck. "Goldie, I swear to God."

"I'm just saying, you've got a really thick—oh, *fuck*." I lose all sense of rational thinking then, because Matty starts to move.

And it's so, so, *so* good. Every thrust is perfect. The way he fills me is, I don't even know, incandescent? Can I describe it like that? Because oh, my *God*.

He rises and tucks my knee against his side, his eyes meeting mine as he pushes into me. "Good?"

"Yes," I breathe. "So, so, *so* good, Matthew."

His eyes flare, and he thrusts again, his abs flexing with every movement, his gaze never wavering. "You feel incredible."

"More," I gasp.

He releases my leg and switches us, still in control as he pulls me on top of him and slams me down on his cock. I cry out, then moan his name as his hands grab my hips. I rock with him, angling the heels away so they don't scratch his legs, rolling to match his own movements, the two of us breathing heavily now.

"There you go," he says. "Take it. Take what you need."

And I do. I take every bit of his cock, riding him like *I'm* the cowboy, my breasts bouncing, feeling strands of hair stick against the sweat on my back.

Before long, I'm panting and sore, my leg muscles protesting a workout they're not used to in the slightest. Matty notices, flipping us again and guiding one of my legs over his shoulder, then pushing in. The angle is perfect, and I groan in pleasure.

"Fuck, Matthew."

He increases his speed, losing all rhythm as we cling to each other. "Goldie," he pants. "Baby, I need you to—"

I shatter, coming apart beneath him with an intensity I've never felt. The world goes black for a second, and I hold onto him with everything I have. Wave after wave rolls over me, cresting again and again, as I mutter an unintelligible string of words.

Matty jerks into me and stills with a groan, his cock pulsing as he comes. We grip each other tightly, our breathing beginning to slow, Matty's head bowed into the crook of my neck. After a moment, I find my voice.

"That was—" I begin.

"Yeah," he finishes. He kisses my temple, then pulls out and gets up to dispose of the condom. He returns in seconds, the two of us working to get under the covers, Matty on his back and propped against a pillow, me draped across him with my head on his chest. We get into the position so quickly that it feels like we've done it for years, not one time.

He tilts his head to mine, and we kiss, lips lingering. "You're staying the night, right?"

I nod. "Wouldn't dream of anything else."

I fall asleep to the sound of his heartbeat.

Chapter 26

Matty

SUNDAY MORNING DAWNS and I wake, turning over and reaching for Goldie, forgetting that I'd worked an emergency shift at the clinic last night and she'd gone home, so we hadn't spent the night at my house like originally planned.

Disappointment crashes through me, followed by a visceral craving for the taste of her, the feel of her beneath me, over me, around me. One night together, and the woman has already caught me so thoroughly in her grip that I can't remember what it's like to want anyone but her.

Killer whines on the floor to the right of me, rising onto his hind legs and pawing at the mattress.

"I'm coming, I'm coming," I mutter, wishing that phrase meant something else entirely right now.

After letting the dogs out—Kitty is more patient than Killer, but not by much—I drop a pod into the coffee maker and start it. Once I have my coffee, I wander outside to the backyard and drop into a chair, relaxing and watching the dogs sniff and play.

Is this really happening? With my *best friend's sister*?

I actually *like* her. All these years, we've kept a line between us that we never crossed. But now that we've moved past the line, I see a woman I never knew: sensual, touching me every chance she gets, and letting me touch her...

I mean, I love her, I've loved her for years as a friend, but this is different. Very different.

I can't say that I'm *in* love with her yet—it's too soon—but the foundation is so strong that of course it's already there.

Is a relationship with Goldie what I want? Because that's exactly where it's heading. We are in the "do not pass go, head straight to relationship" portion of the game here, and I have no idea if that's what I'm after.

Then why did you join the app, asshole?

Okay, fair. I joined the app because I wanted something like what Willa and Reid have. What I didn't expect was to find myself pursuing it with Willa's *sister*. I can admit that I always harbored a fantasy of sorts about her, but it was so unrealistic—and Willa would hate it—that I kept it buried. I take another sip of coffee. Normally, I'd have Willa herself to talk this through, but she's off-limits.

But...is she?

Yes.

She really is. Because as much as she's my best friend, she's Goldie's *sister*, and that takes precedence. And Goldie wanted to keep this quiet while we figure out if this is an actual thing, so we're waiting.

Even though I think this is definitely a thing. Which is terrifying, because I can't imagine her sticking around once she gets to know the real me. If I'm not at the clinic, I'm out at a farm. And if I'm not either of those places, I'm at the diner or home with my animals, reading a book. I used to hang with Willa more, but she's understandably spending time with Reid.

Just as she's getting to know me, the Goldie I'm uncovering is not the same person I've known my whole life. There's far more depth to her than I ever knew. Which sounds terrible—and that's not what I mean. But when it's just us, she gives me pieces of her that I've never seen before. And it's those pieces that make me think that I want more. But what if I let myself want her, and she doesn't want me?

My phone pings and I look down, smiling at the message.

WILLA

Yoga and pier?

It's Sunday. Obviously. Reid coming?

He says he is.

I'm bringing Killer. Yoga studio can't discriminate between small animals.

Even though you promised to keep him at home after the last time? 😏

Yep

lol see you soon

I make myself a light breakfast, then throw on my usual gear for yoga—gear that, for the record, I am never found in if it's not yoga and pier walking.

My phone pings again as I'm loading the dishwasher.

GOLDIE

You wearing those shorts for yoga???

I laugh.

MATTY

Why, you like them?

Are you kidding? •• They're perfection. They've *always* been perfection, and only now am I able to say something about the way they show off your legs.

I feel my cheeks heat.

MATTY

Yes, I'll be wearing the shorts.

[Yes gif from Napoleon Dynamite]

See you there!!

I grab the cloth carrier and scoop Killer into my arms, and we make our way to yoga.

I'm swarmed by just about everyone the second I walk in, but it's not me they're after—it's Killer. It doesn't matter that he's been here before; he's still a tiny dog, and tiny dogs are always going to be a people magnet.

I look up and there's Goldie, hanging back with an unreadable expression on her face. Is it that she's unsure how to act around me, or maybe it's something else? Jealousy?

No way. I should check my ego immediately.

Clearing my throat, I set Killer on the ground to skitter over to Midnight, who's already threading through the mats like the pro she most definitely is. I straighten and meet Goldie's eyes, at a total loss. "Hi."

She smiles. "Hi." Then she looks over her shoulder and back to me. "I, um, saved you a place."

I grin. "Cool." Then I follow her, forcing my attention off her delectable ass and smiling at Willa. When my gaze meets Reid's, he narrows his eyes, and my heart ka-thumps. *Does he know?*

Willa wraps me in a hug. "Hey! How've you been? I've missed you."

I return the embrace, reminding myself that this is my best friend. "Good. I've missed you, too." Then I nod at Reid. "How's it going?"

"Good to see you," he answers, his gaze far too assessing for my taste. Damn police officer. Dude sees way more than a normal person.

Lucky for me, the instructor gives a two-minute warning and I center myself on the mat. Unfortunately for me, I'm next to Goldie, and the session is way more of a turn-on than it should be. The tiny puffs of breath she lets out, the way she moves as we go into pose after pose…I did *not* anticipate this.

We turn and spread our legs to bend over, and I'm faced with Goldie's yellow legging-clad ass and taut thighs. It takes everything I have to suppress the groan that wants to come out. I bite my tongue. As if knowing exactly what she's doing to me, she arches her back, pushing her ass out even more as she breathes into the pose.

I'm going to make her pay for this. I lower my head, knowing good and well I have no business looking at her right now, and stretch into the pose myself. After that, I keep my eyes firmly planted on my mat, my hands, my feet, and the ceiling, because Lord help me if I have to look at the way her skin glistens and know exactly what it tastes like.

After the longest ninety-minute yoga session of my fucking life, Reid and I don the carriers for Midnight and Killer, respectively, and the four of us head out to the pier.

"Let's go check on my boat," Willa jokes, heading toward the line of well-appointed vessels bobbing in the marina. She motions to Goldie. "Tell me how things are going with James."

I stumble. *Shit.*

Goldie flashes me a concerned look and turns her attention to her sister. "It's…good."

"Just good?"

Goldie's cheeks get pink. "Maybe a little better than good."

I've not asked Goldie how much, if any, she's told Willa about the whole Blinding Love app thing, but it makes sense that she's talked about it. And because I'm a glutton for punishment, I ask, "Who's James?"

"You don't know about James?" Reid asks.

"How *would* I know about James?" I counter.

"Just figured you would." His phone goes off and he stops, pulling it out and frowning down at it.

The three of us keep going, and Willa turns her attention back to Goldie. "Any more hot kisses with a masked man?"

Okay, well, *now* I need to hear the whole thing. I lean around Willa and grin knowingly at Goldie. "What's this about hot kisses?"

Willa waves me off as they speed up. "Don't worry about it. We'll go on ahead. You stay back there with Reid or something."

"No way—I want to hear this." I hustle to keep up with them, holding Killer against my chest and leaving Reid in the dust.

"What if I want to hear this?" Reid calls. "I'm a full-fledged small-town resident—I like gossip now, too!"

Willa ignores him and gives me a warning look. "Fine, but I'll remind you that you said you never wanted to discuss anything even remotely like this again after I told you all I wanted was to get some more of Reid's dick."

I barely hold back a retch. "Okay, first of all, you said you wanted—and I quote—'some of that D,' and I was in a vulnerable place back then."

She looks at me skeptically. "What, pray tell, was this vulnerability?"

I try to think of something and fail. "Fine. I didn't want to hear my best friend talk about dick. But this is different."

"I remember this." Goldie laughs, glancing at me. "You looked a little green."

"We're not talking about me," I counter. "Who's James? And is he the masked guy you're having hot kisses with, or is that a different guy?"

Reid appears. "I need the gossip. I have to feed Ox the gossip."

I laugh. "Are you serious?"

"Have you met him?"

"How are he and Anthony related?" Goldie murmurs.

Reid points at her. "Quit avoiding the topic. Give me gossip about kissing hot men in masks. Or hot kisses with men in masks. Whatever." Then he stops. "I can't believe those words just came out of my mouth."

Willa shrugs. "Like you said. You're a full-fledged small-town resident."

"With Ox as your chief of police and best friend," Goldie adds.

"Mask. Kisses. Spill," I command.

Willa whips her head to me. "You're far too into this, you know that?" She narrows her eyes. "Why?"

Reid coughs.

I widen my eyes. "No reason. Just curious. Sounds...fun. Wow, did they paint your boat?" I point to *The Bear*, the biggest yacht in the marina, which Willa claimed the instant it showed up about five years ago.

Willa falls for it and looks, and Goldie catches my eye. The look is half murderous, half appalled, and half something else I can't pinpoint. Yes, that's one and a half. No, I don't care. I'm not at work, so I don't have to make my math be all math-y.

"They didn't paint it," Willa says, a note of disappointment in her voice.

"About this kiss," Reid prompts.

I keep my eyes pointed straight ahead.

"Um, right. I mean, I already told Willa—she didn't tell you?"

"Nope," Reid answers.

And thank God for it, because I'm realizing that it's a damn miracle these two haven't put it together yet. Unless they *do* know and are having way too much fun messing with us.

Goldie clears her throat. "I went to the masquerade ball and kissed a guy in a dark room. It was hot."

Shit. If Reid didn't know before, he *definitely* knows now. My palms are sweaty.

A beat passes. "And?" Reid says. "You gotta give me more."

Willa snorts. "Reid, seriously?"

Goldie huffs. "It's a guy I've been talking to."

"James, right?" *Why am I still talking?* I need to shut up.

She shoots a glare at me. "Right. *Any*way, he pulled me into a dark room, so dark we couldn't see each other. We took our masks off, and…" She trails off, her gaze darting to mine before looking away.

Hell, even *I'm* on the edge of my seat—and I was there. Except I'm waiting on Willa or Reid to put it all together. It'll be like the big reveals at the end of Scooby-Doo, except there's a tiny dog and cat instead of a Great Dane.

Reid clears his throat. "You took your masks off, *and what?*"

Willa smacks him on the arm. "Okay, creeper. That's enough. If she wanted to tell you more, she'd tell you more."

I let out a quiet sigh of relief. Willa would have pounced by now if it was going to happen.

"Fine. But I want to hear more about this James character, so Goldie, if you change your mind." He holds his hand to his ear like it's a phone and mouths, *"Call me."*

Goldie laughs and rolls her eyes. She doesn't seem nervous at all. Meanwhile, all it would take is one well-placed eyebrow arch from Reid and I'd probably break.

"I need to go," Goldie continues, turning to hug Willa. "Call you later?"

"Absolutely."

Reid and I get the usual side-hugs that we always get, and it's not enough. I'm desperate for more, closing my eyes and breathing her in even as she pulls away and smiles.

"Any news on the Bunnies?" I ask, needing to move Reid and Willa far off the masquerade ball topic and hoping that the Miami-based drug cartel that Reid infiltrated before moving to Lucky is a good distraction.

"The main guy's behind bars, but that doesn't mean squat," Reid grumbles. "His daughters are running it now, and they are far more vicious than their father."

"I still want to know where they get the actual rabbits," Willa muses.

I grimace. "Let's not think about that part."

"Hurts your little veterinarian heart, doesn't it?" Reid teases.

I nod earnestly. "It really does. What kind of monster raises rabbits just to, to—" I break off, unable to say it.

"Take their feet and use them as intimidation tactics?" Reid supplies.

I shudder. "Exactly."

My phone buzzes and I pull my phone out to read the text.

GOLDIE

My house. Wear the mask.

I nearly swallow my tongue, then immediately start coughing. Holy *shit*.

Willa gives me some cursory pats on the back. "You okay?"

"Yep," I choke out. "Just, ah, need to go. Great seeing you two." I pivot and head to my truck, tapping out a message.

MATTY

I need a shower and to handle the pets first. Be there in 30.

With the mask

As you wish

Did you just Princess Bride me?

I did. Come to think of it, he wears a mask, too.

Yes. Yes he does.

Wait. Is *that* why women like the movie so much?

Oh, you sweet innocent child.

I'll be there asap

I have never run through a shower and the chores for the pets so quickly. I grab the mask, and the cowboy hat for good measure, then take off.

I send a prayer of thanks that Agatha isn't on her porch as I speed-walk around the house to Goldie's cottage. When I knock, I hear Goldie invite me in.

When I step in, Goldie is nowhere to be found, so I close the door and put on the simple black mask and hat.

"Goldie?"

"In the bedroom," comes the answer.

I force myself to walk through the tiny space, and when I get to the doorway, I stop.

Goldie is on the bed, wearing the black lace mask from the ball, and a yellow, lacy confection that highlights everything wonderful about her body—which is all of it.

CHAPTER 27

MATTY

"GOOD?" SHE ASKS from where she's lying, her smirk telling me that she knows full well she's mimicking me from the other night.

I grin and give her the words she said. "So, so, *so* good, Golden."

She flushes at the nickname, and my cock hardens. "Get naked, Matthew." A beat. "Keep the mask on."

Hell yes. I pull off my boots and socks, then shuck my shirt, pants, and boxer briefs. The hat's gotta go, too, but I leave that until last. Her eyes watch me the entire time, and me? I can't stop looking at her. The way her legs are curled so prettily beneath her, and the yellow lace on her tan skin, the cut-outs designed to draw my eyes to the curves only I get to see. Her tongue darts out to wet her lips, and I groan.

"Spread those thighs, gorgeous." I kneel on the bed as she complies, and a curse leaves my mouth. The outfit she's wearing frames her pussy like the present it is. I bend to her, licking her with languid strokes as her fingers push into my hair, grabbing it and holding me in place.

"There," she gasps. "Please don't stop."

I would never. Not when her muscles are already tensing and she's squirming beneath my mouth. I love that she tells me and shows me what she wants. I love the praise I get when I do it right, too.

"Yes, oh God, *yes*. Matthew, your mouth, holy shit, keep going," she chants above me.

With pleasure. I hold a leg down and press two fingers into her, still licking and sucking her exactly how she wants. She bucks and curses, and I know she's close. Her hands fly above her head to grab onto anything she can reach, and her thighs wrap around my head as she grinds against my mouth, fucking it.

I moan against her pussy, pumping my fingers and curling them against the spot that gets her off. Goldie keens above me, writhing faster and faster as she chases her orgasm. Her clit pulses against my tongue and her walls clench, her moans muffled by the way her legs are tight around my ears.

I could do this forever.

I bring her down slowly as the orgasm wanes, kissing the inside of her thigh and making my way up her body, lavishing attention on every inch of skin the lace reveals. I get to her breasts and feast on one exposed nipple, then the next, my cock painfully hard at the noises this gorgeous woman is making.

She reaches down and grabs my cock, squeezing and pulling exactly how I want it. The sensation is so good I lose focus, and she takes the opportunity to push me onto my back. She straddles my hips, the black mask perfectly in place, her hair wild around It, her incredible body framed by yellow lace, and I nearly lose my mind and come right then.

"How are you real?" I murmur, bringing my hands to her hips. She swirls on top of me, her wet pussy on my bare cock, and I groan. "Careful," I warn, then, "Condoms are in my pants."

She smirks, still gliding against me. "Oh, we don't need one of those yet."

I sink my fingers into her flesh as my eyes roll to the back of my head. "You feel so good." Like silk. Like a dream. Like every fantasy come to life.

"No closed eyes, Matthew," she orders, going onto her knees. "Sit up against those pillows." I do as instructed, and she kneels between my legs, bending toward me to adjust my mask. I bring her closer for a kiss, and she grants it, her tongue moving around mine in a promise of what's to come.

Then she pulls away, kissing and biting her way down my chest to my cock. When her tongue swirls around the head, I nearly come right then.

"Fuck," I hiss. Then I almost black out, because she takes me all the way into her mouth. And I swear, it has never felt this good. Never. Her mouth is velvet and her hands are satin, and she's got me teetering on the edge within seconds. I grab for her, begging my body to hold off, but she doesn't budge.

"Goldie, please," I beg.

She looks up, those beautiful aqua-blue eyes blinking up at me through the mask, and the first thought through my brain is how in the world I missed that it was her that night. Because, of *course,* it was her. How could it not have been? The second thought comes when she hollows her cheeks and sucks, and it's something like, *holy fuck mother of God.*

I yell her name as I crest, losing all sight and sound for a moment and giving myself over only to the feel of her mouth on me, hot and wet and eager. When I come to, gasping for breath and unsure if I'm even back in my body, she's kneeling up, wiping her lips daintily and smiling.

"That was fun," she says.

I bark out a disbelieving laugh. "Yes. Yes, it was. Come here." I open my arms and she folds herself into them. After a moment, I look down and meet her eyes. Her unmistakable eyes. Emotion floods my chest, nearly bowling me over, and thank God I'm lying down. I squeeze her to me.

"Matty?"

"Hmm?"

Her hand glides down my stomach to my dick. "How long before you get hard again?"

On cue, my dick jumps to life. "Apparently, not too long." I shift us and settle between her thighs. "This might be my favorite."

"What is?"

I take her mouth for a kiss, reveling in how soft she goes beneath me, how willing. "Being between your legs."

She smiles, then pulls me back for another kiss. Her mouth opens and our tongues tangle, and when she reaches for me a few minutes later, she smiles against my lips. "Seems like you're ready."

"Stay put," I command, then crawl off the bed to get the condoms in my jeans. When I turn around, her eyes are dark with hunger, and it's intoxicating. I face her as I roll the condom on slowly, letting her get her fill.

"Put the hat back on."

I tilt my head in consent. "Only if you take your outfit off."

In answer, she moves to take it off while I pluck my hat off the floor. I have no idea when it even came off, nor do I care. All I know is whatever Goldie wants, Goldie gets. I settle it on my head and watch as she drops the scraps of lace to the hardwood.

"Tell me what you want."

Her eyes flash behind the mask. "Turn the lights off. Pretend we're back at the ball."

It's daylight outside, so doing it doesn't make the room dark, but I do it anyway. "Come here."

She slides off the bed and walks the few steps to me, gloriously naked except for the mask. When she reaches me, I whip her around, putting her back to my front. She gasps, and my cock throbs against her lower back.

Using one hand on her hip to keep her in position, I sweep hair away from her neck, then trace my fingers down her collarbone and across her chest, circling each breast, moving closer and closer to her nipples with every pass, watching the goosebumps appear in my wake. "You shouldn't be wandering around here in the dark," I whisper, my lips below her ear.

She shivers.

"Look at you," I murmur. "So pretty. So innocent. But now you're here, and I think you're mine." I pinch a nipple and she sucks in a breath. She shifts, her hand aiming to grab my cock, but I move us again, pressing her against the wall and kicking her feet apart. "Ah-ah-ah," I warn, grabbing her hands and sliding them up. "Hands on the wall, gorgeous."

She whimpers. "What are you going to do to me?"

I chuckle darkly. "Ravish you." Then I press two fingers into her pussy without warning.

"Oh my *God.*" Her voice is low, aching with need, and she arches her back to give me better access.

"You always let strangers fuck you with their fingers, pretty?" I release her wrists, pleased that she keeps them in position, then wrap my other hand around a breast and squeeze, my cock hard as fuck.

She trembles as I pump my fingers inside her. She seems already close, and I feel like the king of the world. My girl loves to role-play. I pinch her nipple, rolling it between my fingers and kissing her shoulder.

"You gonna come for me, gorgeous? Tip over into bliss for the stranger with his fingers inside you? Because once you come like this, I'm going to fuck you with my cock."

And just like that, she climaxes, her entire body shuddering, her walls pulsing as I scrape my teeth on her shoulder. I don't let it stop, turning her again and crashing my lips onto hers, still working her hot pussy. She goes onto her tiptoes, then jumps, wrapping her legs around me.

"Please," she mutters, her lips never leaving my mouth as her hips swivel against me. "Please, please, please."

I pull my fingers out to line us up, then push right into her. "Fuck," I groan, her walls gripping me so tight that my knees nearly buckle.

But she's not having it. She grabs the back of my hair and yanks it, forcing our gazes to meet. "Fuck me," she commands. "Fuck me so hard. Make me forget who I am."

Her words set me on fire. I turn us and set her ass on the dresser, then do exactly as she requested, thrusting into her with everything I have.

"Yes, God yes," she mutters, her eyes never leaving mine even as I pound into her. "More. *More.*"

"Fuck," I gasp.

"I need *more.*"

I pull out and grab her off the dresser, and in two steps, I'm dropping her onto the mattress. "Turn over. Give me that ass in the air. *Now.*"

She scrambles into position, presenting herself and looking over her shoulder at me. God *damn,* she's fucking hot.

I kneel behind her and shove in, both of us shouting at the sensation. She takes everything I've got, and I pound into her heat as she pushes against me with every thrust. I lose all sense of reality, knowing only to give her what she wants as hard and fast as possible. Right when she begins to tighten around me, I reach around and find her clit and squeeze.

She detonates.

I'm right behind her.

It's messy, and hot, and the most intense sex of my life.

"Holy fucking shit, Matthew," she says a moment later, breathless. "You can do that to me any time you want."

I laugh. "Yes, ma'am." Then I pull out and handle the condom before collapsing onto the mattress. I remove my mask and throw it, and she unties hers and sets it on the bedside table. I smile. "There you are."

She smiles back affectionately. "There *you* are."

"Come here, Golden."

She snuggles into my arms, and all I can think is that I might want this—want *her*—always.

CHAPTER 28

GOLDIE

IT'S BEEN JUST over a week since Matty and I had what I'm now calling The Sex That Blew Every Other Sex I've Ever Had Out Of The Water, and nothing has changed.

But also: *everything* has changed.

We're at each other's houses almost every night, and when I'm at his, I inevitably end up spending the night. I have a toothbrush there.

I have a toothbrush at Matty freaking Brodigan's house.

I'm still trying to wrap my head around it. It's bliss. On top of that, there's also the constant intrigue of whether we'll get caught, which is both a turn-on and a complete and total stressor. Matty is convinced Reid knows and is letting us stew, and Willa and Mom keep asking when they're going to meet this mystery guy James, and I'm not sure how much longer I can string them along.

TELL US HOW YOU'RE DOING WITH YOUR MATCH!!!

Then there's the app.

The thing keeps asking for updates, and I keep swiping the prompts away. The latest one is in all caps and bold with three exclamation points, as if it, too, wants to know what the hell is going on.

And I don't know.

Because...well, I don't!

It's too much. It's not enough. He's amazing. He fucks me like he took classes on precisely how to make me come multiple ways in multiple positions, and I swear his tongue.

His tongue.

That's it. That's the entire sentence.

Also: his dick.

Matty's thick fucking dick has got me absolutely whipped and I'm *this* close to not caring.

Actually, scratch that: I don't care.

I've been dick-whipped, and I don't care.

I am a staunch feminist who believes in opening my own doors and paying my own way in this world, and I have been utterly and completely whipped by Matty Brodigan's thick dick.

There.

Whew. Gotta say, it feels good to get that out.

Anyway. I need to get my shit together because today I have to see him in a professional capacity. The town council asked me to do portraits of all the business owners in town, and naturally, Matty is the last one standing. The man is ridiculously busy. And that's hot, too, by the way. Seeing him naked and writhing beneath me? Hot. Knowing how smart that big brain of his is, and how caring and patient he is with animals of all types? Scorching.

After my usual morning routine, I load my Jeep with the necessary equipment and head to the clinic. I'm a sweaty mess by the time everything is hauled inside, which would be fine, except that Liv Stinson is behind the counter, smiling and looking like she just stepped out of the glossy pages of a fashion magazine. Never mind that she's in scrubs: I can see every substantial curve she's working with. And her hair and make-up? Flawless.

Matty works with her every day. How has he not dated her? Or maybe they did. Oh, *God*. What if he's…has Liv Stinson had the pleasure of his mouth and fingers and dick?

No. Nope. No, no, no, I can't think like this. Also, I don't *get* to think like this. He had a whole life before me.

Liv flashes a blindingly-white smile at me as I blow a strand of hair out of my face. "Hi, Goldie! You here for Dr. Brodigan?"

Dr. Brodigan. God, even *that's* hot. Did she call him that in bed? *What is wrong with me?* I smile back and answer, "Yes, um…Yes."

Liv looks around, as if searching for an animal.

I lift my camera case. "Portrait time?" I clear my throat. "Sorry. I mean, portrait time. I'm shooting all the business owners. Not, you know, bang bang shooting, but photo shooting."

Her smile falters as I stammer, and in seconds, we're in full-on awkward-as-hell territory. "Right." She draws the word out. "Well, I think Dr. Brodigan has some time between appointments today. Did he—does he know you're coming?"

I nod while my brain helpfully supplies that Matty *always* knows when I'm coming. The flush that covers my entire body is instant. Is it embarrassment? I don't know. All I know is my face is flaming. "Um. Yes. Yes, he knows I'm coming." *Every. Single. Time.*

Liv smiles again, but it's forced. "I'll let him know you're here."

I nod again, my head going up and down like a bobblehead. I point behind me. "I'll just—I'll be over there."

As she stands, I turn away from the counter and wonder where the hell I put my dignity.

A few minutes later, I still haven't found it, but Liv gestures for me to follow her as she walks me to Matty's office. "Will this work? It's not great, but it's all we have."

I force a smile and hope it looks more natural than it feels. "Absolutely."

It's cramped as hell, but if I shove his desk all the way against one wall, I should be able to make it work. Liv leaves, and with a relieved sigh, I get to work.

I'm ready by the time Matty walks in, and my heart stutters to a stop.

He grins as he holds Killer against his chest. "Hi, Goldie."

"Dr. Brodigan," I respond with a rasp.

Of course I've seen him in scrubs. Of course I've seen him in scrubs and boots. I've seen him in boots and a cowboy hat and jeans that I swear were made just for him as he pranced around on a damn horse. I've seen him in that cowboy hat and nothing else, for heaven's sake. But try telling any of that to the rational part of my brain right now.

Because all I see is the *Dr. Matthew Brodigan* in navy script on his white coat and how it hangs over the navy scrubs he wears as he cuddles Killer against him. All I see is the knowing twinkle in his caramel eyes as they trace my body from head to toe and back again. All I see are his hands as he closes the door behind him and stalks toward me, pulling me to him and kissing me like we're not a secret, his mouth claiming me as though he'll keep me forever.

Killer whines between us, and Matty laughs softly as he releases me. "Sorry," he murmurs, "but you look positively delicious when you're in your work element."

I flush. "I could say the same about you."

He smiles, then gestures with Killer to my setup. "So, what are we doing here?"

"Basic stuff, really," I answer. "You'll sit on that stool, and I'll take some shots. With Killer and without him."

He nods agreeably, then takes a seat on the stool. "I'm at your mercy, Goldie."

I lift my camera and click. "Those are precisely the kind of words that can get you in trouble, Dr. Brodigan."

He laughs and I click again. Unsurprisingly, he is the perfect subject, seeming to know instinctively how to angle his body to get the best shot. Killer behaves, as well, and the entire shoot goes by smoothly.

"C'mere," Matty says after he puts Killer down. "Bring the camera."

I make my way to him, sitting on his knee when he pats it in invitation. "Selfies are a lot harder with this," I laugh, but I do my best. When he takes my chin in his hands and turns me softly toward him, I practically feel my insides melting. Because the look in his eyes is enough to quiet all the doubt inside me.

Click.

He kisses me.

Click. Click. Click.

There's a knock on the door. I fly upright and put a respectable amount of distance between us as Matty smirks.

"Yes?" he calls, remaining seated.

Liv pokes her head in, her bright eyes seeming to assess the situation and decide all is well. "Your next patient is here."

Matty nods. "Coco?"

"In exam room one," Liv confirms.

"Five minutes," he says. When Liv's head disappears, he looks back at me. His eyes darken mischievously. "Where were we?"

Click.

He raises an eyebrow.

Click.

"I need those lips, Goldie."

"It's hard not to swoon when you say things like that, you know." I hold my camera up and take one last picture of him as he laughs.

It hits me as I'm loading up my equipment: I'm falling for Matty. Way more than ever before. Before this all started, I'd had a crush on him, sure. But now? *Now* it's way more. It's Cowboy Matty. It's call-me-Golden Matty. It's C'mere Matty. It's thick dicking me down Matty.

If this isn't forever, I'm not sure I'll ever recover.

Chapter 29

Matty

REID

Soooo are you finally going to admit to Ox and me who your mystery girl is or am I gonna have to make this awkward

OX

Wait does Reid know?

REID

Yes Reid knows. Reid most definitely knows, and he has since a certain walk on a pier. AND Matty should be grateful I've been quiet this long.

MATTY

Dammit

OX

Spill it

As Chief of Police I command you to spill it

MATTY

I hate you two

REID

You don't. In fact you're glad that I haven't told
my beloved girlfriend

MATTY

Actually, you're right. I love you. So much. It's
almost unheard of, the love I have for you as my
best friend's boyfriend.

OX

• • • •

REID

Now we're getting somewhere.

OX

I'm dying. DYING.

MATTY

Can we meet for dinner?

REID

Sure how about Dash In Diner

MATTY

Not there for the love of God

OX

Why not? They have the best burgers in town
and Daddy feels like a burger

REID

Ox. My man. I'm gonna have to ask that you
never, on your life, refer to yourself as 'Daddy' in
any chat you and I are in for the rest of our lives

OX

Okay that's fair

Hall's Balls then

MATTY

Fine

It was only a matter of time. If I'm being honest, I'm surprised Reid has let me go as long as he has, because that pier walk was absolutely when he figured it all out. All I can figure is that he's enjoyed letting me sweat.

And I might be. Sweating, that is.

I don't know. I'm confused. Maybe talking to Reid and Ox about everything will be good. Helpful, even. Either way, I've run out of time.

I roll into Hall's Balls at the appointed time and find the guys at the bar, both of them in full police gear. "Are you two even allowed to be in here dressed like that?"

Reid smirks and Ox waves the idea away. "We're on shift. But you aren't. Have a beer." He slides my preferred beer to me as I take a seat.

"How do you want to do this?" Reid asks.

I gulp my beer, then look over at Anthony. "Did they order already?"

Anthony stares back at me.

I nod. Of course they did. "Burger, please." Then, "Did you—did you tell them anything?"

"About what?" Anthony's expression betrays nothing.

"Right. Of course." Dude is a freaking vault.

Ox is damn near wiggling beside me. "Wait—before you say who it is, can I make a guess?"

"Sure."

"It's Liv Stinson." He says it with such confidence, too, all puffed up and certain of himself. He snaps and points at me. "See? Ha! I'm right. It's Liv. All those years working together, the tension off the charts, and then *boom*!"

Reid laughs as I press my lips together and shake my head. "No, man, it's not Liv."

His face falls. "Are you sure? Because the tension there…I feel like it could be. Maybe it *should* be."

"No," I repeat. Is he serious? Liv? My receptionist? *Tension?*

"Can I have another guess?"

"Sure." But honestly, I'm a little worried. "You really thought me and Liv?"

Ox coughs. "Uh, yeah. But you know what? Never mind. That's weird. I'm weird. Sorry. Forget I said anything."

"I'll try." He saw tension with me and Liv? Jesus. I look at Reid. "Should I—"

"Nope," he says. "You should not. Don't think about you and her. Think about you and *her*."

I swallow. "Right. Right!"

Anthony swings back over and pours more tea for Ox. "You know who it is, little brother. Use that head of yours."

Ox's eyes bulge. "*You* know, too? Oh, come on!" he whines. "This isn't fair! How long have you known?"

Anthony shrugs and shoots more water into Reid's glass from the gun.

Ox groans. "This is worse than growing up. You never tell me anything! And you," he glares at Reid. "Sounds like you've known this juicy secret for a while, too. I don't think I like any of you very much right now."

"Well, if that's the case, then maybe we should all leave." Reid stands and grabs my arm.

"No, no, *no* wait!" Ox says, panicked. "I'm sorry. I'll be good. Just, please tell me." He turns his hulking form to me, bending his knees to look me in the eye and raising his hands in a prayer position. "Please?"

I laugh. "You're completely ridiculous, you know that, right?"

Reid nudges me. "Come on. Admit it."

I take a breath, then brace myself. "It's Goldie Dash."

Anthony nods in a way that looks suspiciously like pride. Reid just grins, happy to be right. And Ox? Ox loses his mind.

"What? *What?*" He grips my biceps. "No way! *No. Way!*"

I wince at the man's giant hands on my upper arms. "Um. Ow?"

Ox beams, his face ruddy with absolute joy. "This. Is. Amazing!" He shakes me with every word.

I don't fight it. Who fights an ox? Or, an Ox?

"Holy shit. Holy *shit!* You and little Goldie Dash. This is amazing!" he repeats, looking at his brother, then Reid, then me. His grip, if it's possible, gets even tighter.

"Seriously. Ow." But I'm also laughing, because I have never seen Ox like this. He is absolutely giddy.

"Buddy," Reid says gently, placing a hand on Ox's.

"What? Oh. Sorry." Ox lets me go, but his joy doesn't diminish. Not even a little bit. He crushes me to him in a hug. Which, I gotta say, isn't comfortable. The man is huge, plus he's wearing his bulletproof vest. I pat him in return.

"Okay, Ox. Let the man breathe," Reid chuckles.

Ox releases me once again and I take a deep inhale. "Wow. Oxygen. Good stuff." I take another breath.

"Goldie Dash," he repeats. "Wow. Really?"

I nod.

"Because I always thought...well."

"Enough with Liv Stinson," Reid growls. "What is wrong with you, man?"

"I don't know—I'm an idiot." He hops up on the stool and shakes himself off. "There. All done. No more Liv. We are all Goldie, all the time. Tell. Us. *Everything.*"

Resigned, but also feeling lighter than I have in weeks, I tell them about signing up for the Blinding Love app, and how it matched me with someone named Dawn. How we talked and eventually decided to meet at the Masquerade Ball but didn't reveal who we were.

"Wait," Ox says, his eyes wide. "You were *there*? You couldn't have been. I saw Goldie—she was beautiful. But she was with a cowboy."

I blink, then grin. "The cowboy was *me,* Mr. Chief of Police."

"No." He shakes his head. "That guy's ass was way nicer than yours."

Even Anthony's composure breaks, and we all dissolve into laughter. "Glad to know you think my ass is nice, Ox."

He reddens. "That was *you?* Seriously?"

I shrug. "It's a good suit."

"Clearly," he deadpans. Then he winks at me. "Hat wasn't bad, either."

"Thanks," I say, still chuckling and shaking my head. "But how the hell did you know it was Goldie?"

"Willa knew I was going and wanted me to make sure Goldie was okay. She told me she'd dyed her hair and what she'd be wearing. If it makes you feel any better, she thought I was my brother."

"Liam?"

Ox nods. "I left once I saw Goldie seemed to be having a good time."

Reid leans in. "Oh, I'm told it was way more than a good time."

Ox's eyes go wide. "Ooh, do tell."

Reid looks at me.

I glance over at Anthony, who's slowly moved over and is doing a shit job of pretending to polish glasses and ignore us. He raises an unapologetic shoulder, and I shake my head. Even *he's* a gossip. Glad to know it's a town-wide affliction. Still, there's no harm in giving the masses what they want.

"I pulled her into a dark room and kissed the hell out of her."

Ox swoons. Literally. The man puts a hand on his heart and tosses his head back and *swoons.* "That's so fucking romantic."

I glance at Anthony, who cracks a smile, and I nearly fall off my stool in response. He smirks. "Ox has always been like this, man."

Ox nods. "It's true."

"But you took your masks off first—right?" Reid prompts.

"You're incorrigible."

Anthony slides a fresh beer over.

"The man wants to know," Reid says. "Give our Chief the details."

"Fine. But no more details like that."

Reid holds his hands up. "I don't want to know any more than that."

"Same," Anthony chimes in.

"Girls aren't my jam," Ox adds.

I roll my eyes. "I pulled her into a dark room. I took my hat off, then my mask. Then I took hers off and we kissed. It...was incredible."

"And you really didn't realize it was Goldie?" Ox asks.

"Never," I admit. "But she knew it was me."

"No way," Ox says.

"Really?" Reid says.

"Yep," Anthony answers.

I point to him. "You, my dude, are an eavesdropper of the highest order."

Then *he* winks at me. What is it with the Hall men winking today?

"How does he know?" Reid asks.

I take a deep breath. "Because this is where we met as ourselves. She'd said she knew who I was, and instead of telling me over chat, she suggested we meet here."

Anthony snorts. "He looked like a deer in headlights."

I glare at him. "Not. Helping."

"Maybe he thought it was—" Ox starts.

"*No*," we all chorus.

"Don't make me kick you out," Anthony warns.

"To be fair, I *was* shocked," I admit. "But, shocked in a good way? If that's a thing."

"And now?" Ox prompts.

"Is it serious?" Reid pins me with a look.

"Um..." I hesitate, all my insecurities flooding in at the absolute worst time. I want it to be serious, but I can't shake the worry that she's going to get tired of me.

"Um? *Um?* What is happening right now?" Ox gestures at my open mouth.

"Don't start with me," I shoot back. "You with your *Liv Stinson* mess."

"I'm sorry!" His voice pitches higher than I've ever heard it. "I'm just trying to rewire my brain. Give me a minute."

"You're not giving *me* much of a minute," I huff.

"Just tell us if it's serious," Reid pushes.

I stare at Reid, wanting to answer. But I can't get any words to come. I should be able to immediately say *Yes, this is serious.* But the cold hand of doubt swings from nowhere to grip at my throat, and I swallow thickly. "It's...complicated," I finally manage to say.

Anthony glares at me, muttering under his breath and disappearing to the other end of the bar to serve customers.

Reid's jaw ticks.

Ox gapes. "You're fucking kidding me."

I point at him. "You. Don't talk."

I down my beer. And the one after that.

Chapter 30

Goldie

IT'S MATTY'S NIGHT to come to my house, and I'm finishing up a grilled cheese sandwich and salad at my kitchen table when my phone dings.

REID

Come get your boy

I stare at the text, a vague sense of dread beginning to creep up. I type back with unsteady fingers.

GOLDIE

???

Matty fessed up.

"Holy crap," I whisper. Then I reconsider. Reid's a crafty guy. Maybe this is just his way of ferreting out the truth. Deciding to admit to nothing, I simply repeat my text.

GOLDIE

???

> Cut it out, Goldie. Come to Hall's Balls and I'll give you the rundown.

"Well, shit," I say to my kitchen.

> omw

My hands shouldn't be shaking as badly as they are, but they clearly didn't get the memo. Neither did my legs, because shifting gears in the Jeep is not nearly as smooth as normal.

Ten minutes later, I pull into the Hall's Balls parking lot. I see Matty's truck, and then there's Reid's. And Ox's.

Good Lord. What am I walking into?

I check my reflection in the rearview mirror. I'm flushed and I look like I've been called to the principal's office.

Considering that's exactly how I feel, I'm not surprised.

Yes, I'm twenty-six. And apparently, my people-pleasing tendencies are in full bloom, because right now I want to run and hide until whatever all this is blows over and no one is mad at me anymore.

I blow out a breath. *Here goes nothing*.

I find Matty at the bar between Ox and Reid, with Anthony as bartender like always.

Matty must see something on Anthony's face, because he's the first to swivel around. His smile is sweet and unfiltered...for about two seconds. Then his expression falls, and Reid and Ox turn as one.

"Uh, hi guys!" I try really, *really* hard to sound as normal and unaffected as possible.

"They know." Matty's words are a little fuzzy. "I spilled all the tea."

"Piping hot, too," Ox jokes, but it doesn't meet his eyes.

I study all of them, flitting my gaze to Anthony as well. As usual, his expression gives nothing away. "Okay." I draw the word out. "Everyone knows."

"They know," Matty repeats.

Reid stands. "He can't drive."

I nod, feeling like I'm missing something crucial.

"Give her your keys, yeah?" Ox says softly, tossing bills onto the counter with a nod at his brother.

"Don't act like you care." Matty's voice is ice cold. Then he closes his eyes and exhales, seeming to reset and try again. "I'm not wasted. Of course I'm not driving, but you don't have to act like I'm fragile."

Even still, he pulls his keys out of his pocket and hands them to me. I toss them in my tote.

"This is staying between us." Reid looks at me meaningfully.

"Willa?" I ask.

"Doesn't know—unless you've told her."

I shake my head.

"Between us," he repeats.

Something isn't right. I'm missing something, and it's making me feel like a complete fool. Fighting back tears that have no business showing up and that will absolutely not make themselves known to these men, I draw my shoulders back and beam at Matty. "Ready?"

He nods, and I turn without another word.

I wait for him to climb into the Jeep, then circle around and get into the driver's seat. I start the engine and pull onto the road, unsure what to say. Matty reaches over and tucks a strand of hair behind my ear. "Thanks for coming to get me."

"Anytime." I smile and glance at him, finding him watching me.

He reaches for one of the rubber ducks and holds it up for display. "When did you get this one?"

I look over and see it's wearing a black cowboy hat. Matty

holds it near his face and flashes me a cheesy grin. "Do we look alike?"

I smile, the tightness in my chest dissipating instantly.

I love him.

It's so clear. So painfully clear. Somehow, the knowledge makes whatever happened with Reid and Ox bearable. But I can't tell him. Not right now, when I'm driving and he's not sober.

"Definitely," I answer, clearing my throat and focusing on the road. "Like twins."

He grins happily, then puts the duck back on the dashboard before placing a warm hand on my leg.

At Matty's, I hand him his keys and we head inside for the regular routine: put the dogs out, feed the cats and hedgehog, let the dogs in and feed them.

My chest twinges. All of this feels so…domestic.

"So." I lean against the kitchen counter. "Hall's Balls is where all the good stuff goes down, huh?"

Matty blows out a breath and rakes a hand through his hair. "Something like that, yeah. Let's sit?"

I follow him to the couch, both of us taking up what's become our standard positions: him on one end, me on the other, my feet in his lap, his hands massaging my feet.

"Reid figured us out during that walk on the pier."

I hiss in a breath. "Damn. But he hasn't told my sister?"

Matty shakes his head. "Nope."

If keeping this secret causes trouble with him and Willa, I'll never forgive myself. But I don't say that out loud. "We have to tell her."

His hands still but stay wrapped around my foot. "You're right."

My whole body is tense. Why does this feel so huge? She's my sister. She'll be happy for us. "Together. We tell her together."

He nods and exhales. "Okay. Reid cornered me in a text with Ox."

My eyes widen. "Seriously?"

"Yep. You know how those two love to gossip. Reid threatened to say who it was in the text, but I knew it was better if I told them both face to face."

"You met them at Hall's and, how'd you put it, 'spilled the tea'?" He dips his chin, and I continue. "Why was everyone so weird when I showed up?"

He winces. "Long story?"

I narrow my eyes. "Explain."

He digs a knuckle into my arch, a move so good that my eyes roll into the back of my head. "It doesn't matter," he murmurs. "What matters is that the secret's out, and we're going to tell Willa."

I want to press him, but his hands feel so good on my feet that I can't be bothered. When his hands move farther up my legs, kneading and massaging, I care even less.

He stands and leans down to pick me up, one arm beneath my knees and the other behind my back. I squeal and wrap my arms around him. "Let me take you to bed, Goldie."

I don't hesitate. "Yes, please."

He undresses me with reverence, taking each piece of clothing off and following it with lingering kisses. He divests himself of his own clothes, and when he settles between my legs, the delicious weight of him on top of me, he kisses me like there's no tomorrow. He tunnels a hand through my hair possessively, his other flexing and grabbing me like I'm going to float away.

After he's brought me to orgasm with his mouth, he pushes into me slowly, every inch a decadent torture. His eyes never leave mine, his hips thrusting and swirling as though trying to wring every last emotion out of me. The entire experience feels different, as though he's broken through some kind of barrier.

"Fuck, Golden," he whispers as I come. "You're so fucking beautiful."

It takes everything in me not to tell him I love him.

CHAPTER 31

MATTY

I WAKE UP with my golden girl in my arms.

Because she is. Right?

Fucking Ox. I know he didn't mean anything by it—of course he didn't—but the entire conversation made me sound like an asshole.

Maybe I *am* an asshole.

No. No, what I am is scared.

I get credit for realizing that, right? I have to. It might be all I get in this entire shit sandwich that's been served up on a platter for me.

I'm scared of losing Goldie. So scared. It's not like she's given me a reason to be scared—and if I just *talked* to her, I might find out I don't have a reason to act like this.

But I just…I don't deserve her. Someone as cautious as me, as boring as me, can't possibly deserve a woman as vibrant and alive as Goldie. She's golden. So precious, and sweet, and kind. She sees nothing but the best in people, while I'm…whatever I am… and no way is that good enough for her.

Hell, *no one* is good enough for her.

And sure, I know that she's the only one who can decide

who's worthy, and I shouldn't be making that decision for her, blah blah blah. But let's not kid ourselves: if I couldn't immediately answer Reid last night when he asked if it was serious, then do I really have any business wasting her time?

She shifts a little, just enough so I can roll out of bed without disturbing her.

I tiptoe out of the bedroom and begin the morning ritual: let the dogs out, start the coffee, feed the cats, let the dogs in, feed the dogs, feed the hedgehog. I pull out the vanilla creamer I've started keeping at the house for her.

I'm so lost in my thoughts, making breakfast I don't know I'll even be able to eat, that I don't hear Goldie come into the kitchen. And when her arms wrap around me and she kisses my shoulder, the absolute worst thing in the world happens: my body stiffens.

And there it is.

If my own body can't be trusted to react appropriately, then I have no right to her. None.

She releases me immediately, and a beat later, she appears at my right, pouring a cup of coffee and putting way too much vanilla creamer in it, just the way she likes it. She doesn't speak.

I plate our eggs just as the toast that she started pops out. We meet at the table, still silent, until finally she breaks.

"What's going on?"

I look up at her. She's looking at me with wide open eyes. They're so innocent.

I'm such a fucking asshole.

"Matty?" she prompts again.

"I—" I blow out a breath. "I can't do this."

"Can't do what?"

I blink, unwilling to believe I let the words come out.

"You just said you can't do this," she continues, setting her fork down. "Can't do what?"

A noise blares in my head, like what I imagine a tornado

might sound like. I've never heard one, but I read somewhere once that they sound like trains. And it feels like I'm standing in front of one, waiting on it to run me down. A train, a tornado: it doesn't matter. Both are going to decimate me.

"Matthew James Brodigan." The words are supposed to sound harsh, but they don't. They simply sound like a plea. "Tell me what you can't do."

Finally, I find my voice. "Us." But the word cracks when it comes out. I try again. "I can't do us."

She breathes in tiny gasps of air, then reaches for her coffee. Lifts it, sets it down as if it weighs too much. Brings her napkin to her mouth, lays it on the table next to the eggs she never even cut into. Exhales.

"I'm…" But I stop. I'm *what?* I'm sorry? I'm scared? I'm an asshole? I'm kidding? There's nothing to say. It's done.

"Why?"

I meet her eyes. All I can do is repeat her question. "Why?"

She nods, blinks rapidly. When she speaks, her voice is watery. "I deserve as much, don't you think?"

"Because…" I breathe. This shouldn't be so hard. *Fuck*, the sound in my head. I need it to stop. If it would just stop, maybe I could think. Maybe I could make sense of all of this.

"Right. Got it." She scoots her chair out and stands without another word.

I watch her leave the room, and suddenly, I'm angry. She doesn't want to fight for us? Fine. We clearly don't mean that much to each other if she can't even be bothered to push for a reason. To push for answers. Maybe if she pushed, I could find the words. Hasn't she been the one taking the lead this whole time? And now, when I really need her to step up, she doesn't?

Ox's proclamation that he always thought it would be me with Liv Stinson, of all people, was bad enough. But seeing Goldie's reaction? That's the ultimate sign.

We have to stop before we ruin everything.

A few minutes later, Goldie appears in the kitchen, an over-stuffed tote on her shoulder and Kitty and Killer prancing around her legs, vying for attention. My heart nearly stops. What am I doing?

"I think I have everything here. But if I've missed something, just..." She doesn't finish the sentence.

I keep my eyes on my plate as she walks past. I want to grab her hand and beg her to stay. To go to my knees and tell her I'm an idiot. That I'm scared and I know I don't deserve her, but I'll do whatever I need to do to convince her to stay with me forever.

But I don't. I remain perfectly still.

And if I breathe deeply, hoping for one last inhale of her sunshine scent because I have no idea the next time she'll even deign to be in the same room with me, then so be it.

CHAPTER 32

GOLDIE

Figures that my own sister won't let me take a day off. It was easy to convince JJ to leave me alone the past few days, but Willa? No such luck.

I pull on jeans and a T-shirt and brush my teeth, but she's got another thing coming if she thinks I'm going to brush my hair and put on makeup. There's only so much I can be expected to do with a broken heart.

Because yes, Matty fucking broke my heart. That asshole wormed his way in, perfectly content to have me as his little secret. But when the news got out and he had to face reality?

Poof. Done.

I swipe at the tears and start my Jeep, then see the cowboy duck on the dashboard.

…And the tears come in earnest now. I slump in the seat, powerless to fight them. I've been crying for over forty-eight hours now, so what's another few minutes?

Finally, I pull myself together with a hiccup. He's not an asshole. He's just…stupid.

Really, really stupid.

When I get to the diner, Mom's already there and wiping down the menus. "Goldie!" she gasps, grabbing my arms and leading me to the counter. "Honey, what happened?" She leans in and lowers her voice. "Is it James?"

Willa looks through the serving window from where she stands in the kitchen, chopping onions. "Goldie?" Her brow furrows when she sees me.

I swallow hard and wave them both away. "Don't worry about it. I'll be okay."

Willa's face softens. "Do you need to go home?"

I shake my head, realizing that home is actually the last place I want to be. Every room makes me think of Matty. "No." I sniff. I stand and grab the silverware and napkins, then start rolling the silverware. I need to lose myself in anything that isn't thoughts of him, and this is the perfect way to start.

Mom rubs my back but doesn't push for details, which is honestly a miracle. I must really look like shit.

Tom and Jerry make their shuffling way in as soon as Mom flips the sign to Open and unlocks the door. I pour their coffees.

"The heck happened to you, girlie?" Tom asks. "You look terrible."

Jerry swats him. "You're not supposed to comment on how a woman looks, Tom!"

"Since when?"

"Since forever," Jerry shoots back. "Have some manners."

"I have manners. Watch this." Tom turns to me, one of his suspenders slipping off his flannel-checked shoulder. "Goldie, dear, your bedraggled state and lack of smiles indicate that you are in distress. How may we assist? Is there someone to whom we need to defend your honor?"

Willa snorts behind me, and despite my sorrow, the tiniest of smiles makes its way onto my face.

"Good Lord," Jerry moans, then turns his attention to me. "Ignore him. You're allowed to look however you want to look. And if that means wearing clothes that even Willa wouldn't be caught in, and wearing your hair like, well, whatever that is, then you go for it. Girl power!" He raises a shaky hand halfway into the air, which I'm pretty sure is as far as it'll go.

"I heard that," Willa says behind me.

"Do you honestly think that was better than me?" Tom asks Jerry. "Get some class."

"I've got class—it's why Sue agreed to date me instead of you."

"Only because I told Sue I felt sorry for you!" Tom sputters.

"Are you lying about my wife?" Color rises on Jerry's cheeks. "My beloved? Outside, sir!"

"Ach, get over yourself." Tom waves Jerry's threats away and looks back at me. "We're here if you need us."

I pat both their hands as Jerry continues to mutter. "Thank you both. You're very kind."

More customers begin to arrive, and I lose myself in the shift, thankful for how busy it gets and even more grateful that Matty himself doesn't show up.

Ox and Reid do, however, and I send yet another prayer of gratitude to the diner gods when they go to the counter instead of sitting at the open table. All I have to do is avoid them, and all will be well.

"Goldie." Ox's voice is soft and gentle as I walk past, and against my better judgment, I turn to him.

"Hi, Ox. You doing okay?"

"I've been better."

I peer closer. He actually doesn't look so well. Smudges of purple beneath his eyes hint at a lack of sleep, and he's got days-old stubble. "What's going on?"

Reid touches my elbow and looks at Ox. "She needs to work, Ox. This isn't the time."

Ox shakes his head, his hulking form seeming to deflate before my eyes. "I know, but I—" He stops and looks up at me. "I'm so sorry, Goldie. It's all my fault."

I look between him and Reid, confused. "I don't understand."

Reid blows out a breath. "It's not your fault, Ox. If it's anyone's, it's probably mine. I'm the one who asked him if it was serious."

My body goes hot. "You *what?*"

"I'm the one who said it was Liv Stinson!" Ox exclaims.

I swivel my glare to Ox. "You...*what?*" I repeat, gritting my teeth. Fucking Liv Stinson.

"Reid made Matty spill everything at the bar, and we might have all said some things we regret," Ox says, his words fumbling out. "And now you're here looking sad, Matty won't talk to us, Willa's irritated no one will tell her what's going on, and it's our fault."

Horrified, I look at Reid. "You *still* haven't said anything?"

"I told you I wouldn't. It's obvious I messed things up enough; no way was I going to go tell your sister your business. Especially when it seems like things are...bad."

I don't know if I should laugh, cry, or scream.

I *do* know that the tears are coming.

I whirl away from them and untie my apron, shoving it at Mom. "I'm sorry," I choke. "But I can't."

"What in the world?" Mom asks, her eyes wide and searching as she takes the apron. "Honey?"

I don't answer, barging into the kitchen and moving through it to the back office. Only when I'm in there and the door is shut do I let go. Tears stream down my face as I try to make sense of what Reid and Ox just said.

No. It doesn't matter. Whatever they said or didn't say, the fact is that Matty made his own decision.

A knock comes at the door and Willa comes in, a chef's knife in her hand. "What's going on?" she demands.

I make a feeble attempt at wiping the tears away, and wave at her hand. "Put down the knife and I'll tell you."

She startles and looks down. "Oh," she says sheepishly. "I didn't know I still had it."

"Why does that not surprise me?" I murmur.

She sets the knife down and sits in the chair opposite me. "Is this about James?"

I meet her eyes. I know we said we'd tell her together, but that was before he ripped my heart to shreds. "It's about Matty."

She blinks. "Matty? What did he do?"

Tears flood my eyes again as I say, "He broke my heart."

"Are you *sure* I don't need my knife?" she asks, not skipping a beat.

I laugh and grab a tissue from the box on the desk, then blow my nose. "No knife. Not yet, anyway."

She grunts. "We'll see about that. What did my best friend do to my baby sister?"

On a sigh, I admit it. "It was always him, Willa. James. James *is* Matty."

Her jaw hits the floor. "Oh my God. Come here." She pulls my hand until I'm up and sitting in her lap, and her arms wrap around me and squeeze.

My tears come even harder as I squeeze her back. "It hurts, Willa. So much."

She rubs a soothing hand in circles on my back and lets me cry, because she is the best sister in the history of sisters.

"I should have told you as soon as I knew. I'm so sorry," I sniff.

Still holding onto me, she reaches for the box of tissues and brings them closer. "I don't care. That had to be a lot to carry, though. For both of you."

I straighten to blow my nose again and nod, finally meeting her eyes. My voice is tiny and small when I say, "He's being a stupid, scared asshole."

Her mouth quirks up. "Doesn't surprise me in the least. Do you want to tell me what happened?"

I sit back in my own chair, and ten minutes later, she's heard everything.

"How dumb can he possibly be?" she seethes.

I smile sadly and toss a crumpled tissue in the trash can. "You're not mad?"

"Why would I be mad?"

"That your best friend and little sister were dating."

She reaches for my hand and squeezes. "Nevers. You like who you like. Am I sad that you didn't think you could talk to me about it? A little, but that's okay. You know," she muses, "Reid thought you two had a thing when he first got here."

I shrug. "Reid and Ox are involved, too. Reid figured it out when we were at the pier, and after he and Ox talked to Matty, that's when Matty called it off. But I'm still not exactly sure what happened, and I don't blame those two."

Willa grunts as she stands and grabs the knife. "I need to talk to Reid."

I wince. "Maybe not with a sharp object in your hand?"

She raises an eyebrow. "We'll see."

MATTY

WILLA

I expect you at yoga and a walk.

MATTY

I'm not really up to it

I don't really give a shit, Matthew. Yoga. Walk.
You and me. Alone.

K iller licks my face as I stare at her text, and I have a feeling she's dead serious. "You know what, little guy? Miss Willa has been awfully bossy these last months." He barks and licks my face again. "I guess we have Reid to blame for that. Or thank."

The chihuahua hops off my lap, yips, and heads to the back door. I stand up. "I know. We thank him. Even if we're a little scared of Willa right now. You wanna go out?"

He prances in a circle, his nails tapping on the hardwood. Kitty watches dispassionately from his bed in the corner, clearly not sharing Killer's need at this time.

On a sigh, I let him out and get ready for yoga. To be honest,

I've not felt like doing anything these past few days. All I can see are Goldie's eyes. The way they blinked so innocently at me, then seemed to empty of all emotion when she realized I wasn't going to speak.

Why didn't she fight for us?

My stomach aches with guilt. That's not the question I should be asking, and I know it.

I arrive at the appointed time, Killer wrapped in his usual carrier around my chest, and find Willa waiting for me outside the studio. "Let's go." She points toward the pier.

"No yoga?"

"No."

"O-kay," I say, trying to feel her out.

She doesn't speak as we walk, but it's clear she's getting more and more pissed. Once we're out on the pier, I decide there's nothing to do but dive on in. Metaphorically, that is. "You wanted to talk?"

She stops and whirls on me. "What in the actual *hell* have you been thinking?"

"Me?"

She pokes my chest. "Yes. *You*, Matty. Or should I call you James?"

I exhale. "You know."

"Did you think I wouldn't?"

Head hanging, all I can say is, "Shit."

She pokes me again. "Yeah. Shit. You're lucky we're not at the diner. There are no knives around here."

I back away. "Jesus, Willa."

"Oh, no way, buddy. You don't get to act all offended or worried. What. Were. You. Thinking?" she growls.

I wipe a hand down my face. "I...wasn't?"

"You're damn right you weren't!" She swivels and stomps away, then stomps back. "Seriously, Matty, how could you be so *stupid*?"

And *that's* the question I should have been asking myself these past four days. Problem is, there's no answer. "I'm...not sure what you want me to say."

She throws her hands up. "What do I want you to say? What I *want* is for you to start at the beginning and explain to me what happened!"

"I didn't know it was her at first—"

"But then you *did*. And you acted like a certifiable asshole!"

I blink. "Wait. Wait, wait, wait."

She crosses her arms and levels a look that I didn't think she was capable of. I am officially terrified for any children she may have, because holy shit. "I'm waiting, Matthew."

Suddenly, my mouth is dry. "Right. Okay. Can I clarify something first?"

"Sure. Who knows? It might even help your case."

"Are you mad because I was dating her? Or—"

Willa scoffs. "Since when is that a big deal? I know I told you to consult your romance novels when you told me there was something 'complicated' going on with a woman, but I didn't tell you to take the novels to be actual reality."

"Meaning..."

"Meaning I don't care that you were dating Goldie. What I *do* care about is that you broke her heart, you idiot!"

I frown. "What?"

She thumps my forehead.

"Ow!"

She thumps it again. "You deserve more than that. You are so dumb, Matty. That girl has had eyes for you since forever. I mean, believe me, I wish she hadn't. Especially the way you're acting now."

"Hey," I protest, but she keeps going.

"I ignored her crush for a *long* time, and you did an immaculate job of being totally clueless, too."

I've had it. "Okay, that's enough. She did not have some lifetime crush on me. That's insane. She's…Goldie. I was the skinny nerd hanging out with her older sister. Why would she like me, of all people, her whole life?"

Willa groans in frustration and moves to thump my forehead a third time, but I swat her away. "Yes she did, Matty! She even told you so, you stupid, stupid man. *Think.* She's always looked at you like you hung the damn moon. Is it any wonder that when the app put the two of you together, she was going to hold on for all she was worth?"

"I just—"

"What? What? Are you only now realizing what a complete and total jackass you've been? Because believe me, I can list *all* the fucking ways."

I flinch. Willa doesn't really cuss, so hearing her do it is jarring. "Um."

She holds up a finger. "You made her feel special." Another finger. "The two of you do…all sorts of things that I do *not* want to hear about, and have all but told each other you love each other." A third finger. "You act like a baby when Ox's idiot self names your receptionist as the woman he thinks is the love of your life." A fourth. "You *can't answer* when Reid asks if it's serious." A thumb. "And then, you tell her 'you can't do this?' Are you out of your *fucking mind?*"

I duck. Because Willa is coming for me fast and furious, her open hands slapping my arms and head one after the other as she cusses me out. Even Killer gets into the game, yipping and wiggling as if he, too, is profoundly disappointed in me. "Okay, okay!" I holler, covering my head. "You're right! I love her!"

She keeps whacking me, each word punctuated by an open palm on my bicep. "You're. Not. Acting. Like. It!"

"Of *course* I love her!" I yell. I pull in a deep breath of air and back away from her again. "How could I not? She's everything, Willa. Everything. She is the sun, the moon, and everything in between. *Fuck.*"

Willa beams. "Finally."

I straighten and make sure Killer is good. I pat his head as he snuggles back against me. "Finally?"

"Yes. Finally."

And it hits me.

I love her.

I *love* her.

And she loves me. Or at least, she did.

And wow, have I been a complete and total ass—just like Willa said.

"Oh no."

She smirks. "Yeah. Oh no. God, you're so fucking stupid." She jerks her thumb at a bench, and we sit. "Now, are you going to tell me why you acted like such a jerk in the first place?"

I hook a small leash on Killer and let him down to sniff, then study the ocean. "I'm not worthy of her."

Willa snorts. "No shit. What else?"

"Isn't that enough?"

"No one is worthy of my sister, Matty. There's more to it than that." She slides her gaze to me. "Is it your parents?"

Her question is a merciless arrow hitting its target, and I wince as it digs into place. "Maybe."

She's quiet, letting me stew in my own pot of emotions, but when she opens her hand on the bench beside me, I thread my fingers through hers and relish the comforting squeeze.

"Did you know they thought I was boring?" I finally say. Her hand squeezes tighter, giving me the strength I need to keep talking. "Said it more than once. And I don't think they meant it to be cruel, I think they thought they were making a joke. But it...I guess it dug deep. Even though I told them I didn't care if I was boring. And when they left town, it didn't hurt like I thought it would. Like I thought it *should*."

"Your parents are idiots," Willa says softly. "You've brought nothing but excitement and color into my life, Matty. I can't imagine growing up without your underground kitten ring, or the summer we spent mowing lawns because you wanted to use the money to adopt all the animals at the shelter, or the months we spent talking like pirates." She laughs. "And now, you're a cowboy."

"I am not," I smile weakly.

"But how does all this come back to Goldie?" she prompts.

I sigh. "I'm scared that she'll realize I'm not nearly as interesting and amazing as she is. That she'll wake up one day and decide I'm not exciting enough. That I'm some weak, nerdy vet who spends more time with cows than humans sometimes. And I might miss things because of animal emergencies—big, important things."

"But all this is conjecture, babe. If Goldie's deemed you worthy, then shouldn't you believe her?"

"I've really fucked up, haven't I?"

Her smile is rueful. "You're not in a great place. But all hope isn't lost."

I look at my best friend, utterly helpless. "What do I do?"

"Don't look at me," she says, then smirks. "Maybe your buddies can help."

CHAPTER 34

MATTY

MATTY

I NEED help.

REID

Have you come to your senses yet?

OX

I don't help idiots so if you haven't then remove me from this chat

MATTY

Not a lot of room for you to talk there, buddy. But yes, I have.

REID

...

OX

...

MATTY

Are you two sitting next to each other giving me crap?

REID

Maybe

OX

We'll never tell

MATTY

How do I make it up to her?

OX

To whom?

REID

That's some fancy language for an Alabama boy

OX

Shut up Florida Man

REID

That's a low blow

OX

If the shoe fits

MATTY

Can we focus?

OX

Still waiting on you to tell us who you're talking about

MATTY

GOLDIE you fools

REID

I don't think you're in a position to call us names

OX

Actually if anyone is the fool it's Matty

MATTY

Ox, you need to look in the mirror.

OX

Oh I did. I look amazing. I look like I didn't
mess up.

MATTY

Fine. *I'm* a fool. I'm a fool for Goldie. I'm a fool
in love with Goldie. And I need to figure out a
way to tell her. Like, making it front page news
worthy.

REID

You mean you never told her you loved her?

OX

Good Lord

MATTY

You have no room to talk Reid. Took you nearly
getting killed by Ted Thompson before you came
to your senses.

OX

Wow, coming in hot!

REID

Old news.

MATTY

You know what? Forget it, I'll figure this out on
my own and leave you clowns out of it.

OX

REID

I have an idea.

OX

You do?

REID

Of course I do.

MATTY

I can't decide if I'm relieved or terrified.

OX

Both is probably the way to go.

REID

Do you trust me?

MATTY

Do I look like someone who has a leg to stand on?

OX

Look at you, figuring it all out. I'm so proud.

MATTY

I'm still waiting on an apology from you, Ox.

OX

You did it to yourself

REID

I need a horse and a river.

MATTY

Welp. Now I know the answer: Terrified

OX

The answer is EXCITED, Matty. Excited.

MATTY

You already know what it is, don't you?

OX

I mean, we *are* sitting next to each other. Did you know that Reid uses Talk to Text?

MATTY

Learning something new every day.

REID

Focus, you two. I have a plan.

OX

And it is so good. If he weren't straight…

REID

Aw, I love you, too.

MATTY

REID

Call me when you have a spot.

MATTY

Me? Or Ox?

REID

Why would Ox need to call me?

MATTY

I don't know. I'm confused.

OX

Call him. The idea is good.

MATTY

Give me an hour.

T click the screen off and take a deep breath, then blow it out. Killer's head pokes out from the blanket he's cuddled in on the couch, his out of proportion ears on high alert. "Just me, buddy." He looks around, huffs, and drops his head onto the blanket. I swear, he might miss Goldie more than I do.

It's taken me longer than I'd like to come to my senses, but I'm here now.

The app dings.

TELL US HOW IT'S GOING WITH YOUR MATCH!!!

I glare at it. How's it going? The temptation to rate the app zero stars is high, let me tell you. But I'm better than that. And it's not like this is the app's fault. The app did exactly what it was supposed to do.

And speaking of doing what is supposed to get done, I pick up my phone and dial. When I finish that call, I make a second one.

THE NEXT DAY, REID AND I ARE IN MY TRUCK ON THE way to Farmer John's. "You ever ridden a horse?"

Reid shakes his head. "Do I look like the kind of guy who's spent time on one?"

I snort. "No, but that doesn't mean much. You could have done it when you were a kid at a camp or something."

"Nope. You ready for this?"

"I just need to know that you're good with a camera."

Reid holds up the bag. "It's pretty self-explanatory. Point, shoot. Also," he holds up his phone, "this is pretty foolproof. Especially once I get the thirst-trap videos of you I'm planning on."

I shift in my seat. "Yeah, about that."

"Oh, don't even *think* you're getting out of it. I promise you, it's going to work."

"But JJ and I have written a whole article."

Reid blows a raspberry. "Article, shmarticle. She's not going to care about the words once the video plays."

We pull up to the farm half an hour later, and I grab my vet bag out of habit.

Reid eyes it. "Yes—I like the way you think. We'll get some videos of you shirtless and checking on animals."

I stop. "Exactly how much of this idea was yours versus Ox's?"

Reid laughs. "Exactly *none* of this was Ox's. And remember—

you're the one who said you needed to make it front page news-worthy. I'm just working with what I've got."

"You mean what *I've* got." I smile.

Reid snaps and points at me. "Now you're catching on."

Farmer John meets us at his barn, and I make the intro-ductions.

John shakes Reid's hand. "Aren't you the guy who was in that bunny ring?"

Reid chuckles. "Not exactly a bunny ring, but yes. That was me."

John nods. "Well, let's get you on a horse, Doc." He turns and we follow him into the barn and to the second stall on the right.

There's a gorgeous brown horse in there, and I smile broadly. "I get Peppermint?"

Peppermint's ears tip forward as she extends her neck and leans down to sniff me. I produce the mints the horse is named after, and she takes one, then two, out of my palm with velvety lips. I laugh and rub her nose with my free hand. She was the first horse I helped bring into this world, and I've been in love with her from the beginning.

"Good girl. You've gotta help me look like I know what I'm doing, okay?"

She eyes me, then leans to sniff my pockets once more. John helps to get her tacked up, then points out the shortest route to the creek.

Reid looks around. "Got any way for me to get there?"

John nods. "Had a feeling a city boy like you wouldn't be riding a horse. I've got the four-wheeler gassed up. But you need to keep a healthy distance between you and Peppermint. She's a great horse, but she's not much of a fan of the things."

"Fair enough."

Half an hour later, Reid's got me splashing Peppermint through the creek, shirtless, while he snaps picture after picture.

"Do it again! Only this time, look sultry."

I laugh. "Fuck you, sultry. How do I do that?"

"Like this." Reid lowers his camera and levels me with a look that is nothing short of scorching.

"Damn, dude." I whistle. "You sure you've not been an underwear model or something? Calvin Klein calling?"

He winks, then holds the camera up. "Come on. I won't make fun of you, and I promise not to show Ox the bad ones."

"That's...not very comforting." But I do what he says.

CHAPTER 35

THE LUCKY DAILY

SPECIAL EDITION PRINTING

IS TRUE LOVE REALLY BLIND?
BY NOLAN "JJ" JENKINS

Citizens of Lucky, have I got a treat for you. And for once, I didn't have to go chasing this story down for you: It came right to me.

And by story, I mean Dr. Matthew Brodigan.

And by Dr. Matthew Brodigan, I mean Matty B. Although I'm pretty sure no one's called him that since high school.

Anyway.

Many of you may not know that there are an absolute plethora of dating apps out there. I personally have not engaged with any of these apps, but a cursory glance shows, well, a lot. And I'm told that anyone who's single can tell you all about them, and while I'm single, I am not, in fact, one of those people who can tell you all about them.

I'm losing focus again. I clearly have not had enough time to edit this piece. But that's what happens when the town's vet, chief of police, and newest police hire come swinging into this editor's house and demand I do…whatever it is I'm doing.

Anyway, have you read this far? Good for you. Congratulations.

It turns out that Matty Brodigan, Dr. Matthew to you kids, has been dating one Goldie Dash.

That's right: Matty and Goldie.

Sitting in a tree

K-I-S-S-I-N

Good Lord, what is *wrong* with me? No one's actually reading this in physical form. Right? You're watching the video online. You *have* to be watching the video.

Goldie, it's Matty. I took the laptop away from JJ. He's sweating. It's…not a good look. I think Reid scares him? Reid just read this over my shoulder and laughed and said yes, he definitely scares JJ, and he likes it that way.

Back to us: I messed up. It's as simple as that.

I was a complete and total idiot. And your sister—who, for anyone else reading this, is incidentally my best friend—was more than happy to tell me just how badly I messed up, too. I think even Killer read me the riot act.

I was terrified.

What we had seemed too perfect, you know? It didn't seem possible that I could have it all: you *and* everything else? No way could I be that lucky. I couldn't shake that doubt, even from the beginning.

First, I thought Willa would be mad.

For the record? She doesn't care. But you know that already. She's mad that I hurt you. She's mad that I didn't give her enough credit. I don't blame her.

I love you.

I love you so much, and I want to spend the rest of my life making it up to you for being so stupid.

I have more to say, but I'd rather say it in person. So here goes:

If you're willing to give me a chance, then meet me tomorrow at ten a.m. at the clock in town square.

I love you.

P.S. Reid says to enjoy the pictures and video.

P.P.S. JJ wants to remind the readers that the video is online. There's no video on the actual paper. Seriously, JJ? No shit, man. This is real life. Not some fantasy or sci fi show where pictures move on paper.

P.P.P.S. I love you, Goldie. Please be there.

CHAPTER 36

GOLDIE

I ROLL OVER and cover my head with the pillow, drowning out the incessant construction that seems to be happening outside my house.

Thump thump thump

"Goldie!"

I pull the pillow off. Is that someone—?

"Goldie Dash, you answer your door this instant!"

I sigh. Agatha better have a real good reason for waking me up. I was having an incredible dream. Matty's head was between my thighs...

"Goldie! *Hurry!*"

"One second!" I call, getting up and shoving my feet into my slippers, then donning my glasses and grabbing my phone out of habit. I squint at the screen.

Is that...thirty notifications?

What is going on?

I speed up, racing to the door and flinging it open.

"Goldie!" Agatha's waves *The Lucky Daily* at me.

"Ahh! What?!" I wield my phone like it's a magic sword, ready to take down my enemy.

"You're going to be *late!*" she yells, then heaves herself over the threshold and shoves me to the side as she goes. "Get dressed!"

"What is happening?" I yell back. "Why are you yelling?"

She waves the paper once more and keeps walking to my bedroom. "Go online to *The Lucky Daily* website. Who sleeps this late?"

"I had a late night," I whine, but she's out of sight and shouting at me to hurry up.

Unlocking my phone, I ignore the notifications and go straight to the paper's website.

"Holy crap." I stop mid-stride, gaping at the screen.

Matthew James Brodigan filmed a freaking thirst trap.

He's shirtless and sweaty, walking toward the camera with a damn horse, wearing that hot-as-sin cowboy hat and jeans that were made for him…

And it's in slow motion.

"Oh my God."

I watch it again.

I might be drooling.

"What are you *doing*?" Agatha appears in front of me.

I startle, nearly dropping the phone but fumbling it and getting it upright just in time to watch the video again. "Matty. He made a—"

"You're going to be late to *meet* Matty if you don't come *on!*" She grabs my free hand and yanks me to the bedroom. "Get dressed."

"I'm still not sure what's going on."

She rolls her eyes and shoves the print copy of the paper at me. "You have three minutes, missy, and not a second more."

Immediately my eyes snag on the pictures of Matty—more shirtless, gorgeous pictures—but then I see the headline: Is True Love Really Blind?

"What *is* this?" I mutter, skimming the initial paragraphs.

Then I get to Matty's words and suck in a breath. "Agatha." I shoot my hand out and grab her shoulder.

"Told you," she sniffs.

"I love you. I love you so much, and I want to spend the rest of my life making it up to you for being so stupid. I have more to say, but I'd rather say it in person. So here goes: If you're willing to give me a chance, then meet me tomorrow at ten a.m. at the clock in town square."

I look at the time. "Oh my God!"

"Now you're catching on."

"It's nine fifty-eight! Agatha! *Agatha!"* I turn in circles, unsure what to do. "I go, right?"

"Of *course* you go! Get dressed!"

My body flushes with heat. "You keep saying that! I don't have time!"

"Yes you do! *Hurry!"*

Without thought, I haul myself to the dresser and throw on a skirt, then a shirt. "I need to brush my teeth!" I push past Agatha. "Shoes are in my closet!"

"On it!" she replies. "Keys?"

"Bowl by the door!" I shove the toothbrush in, give my teeth maybe five seconds, swish, toss another blob of toothpaste onto my tongue for good measure, then run out. I shove my feet into the shoes Agatha's set out—not at all what I would have picked, but whatever—and grab the Jeep's keys from her hand.

"I'll lock up. *Go!"*

But I pause for one precious moment, taking her in, trying to wrap my head around what's happening. "Thank you," I say, leaning to give her a hug.

She lets me hug her for all of two seconds before shoving me toward the door with a smile. "Get out of here! Go get your guy."

I take off running.

CHAPTER 37

GOLDIE

T'S ELEVEN MINUTES past ten when I screech into a space at the park and kill the engine.

I'm late.

What if he's not here?

My stomach roils, and I shove it all down. I can't think about that. He has to still be here. He *has* to. I jump out of the Jeep and run into the park, side-stepping way more people than it seems would normally be here on a weekday morning. Don't these people have jobs?

Doesn't matter.

"Matty!" I call as I get to the clock a moment later, looking around. He's not here.

And that damn clock shows I'm fifteen minutes late.

"Matty!" I probably sound like an idiot, but never have I cared less. "Where are you?"

There. I catch a glimpse of a black cowboy hat on the far side of the park as the person walks out of sight. That has to be him. I break into a sprint, waving my arms and yelling his name. *Please.*

He turns.

It's him.

I keep running, eating up the distance between us as he slowly begins to walk my way.

"Goldie?" The faintest of smiles appears on his handsome face.

"Matty!"

Finally, *finally* I get to him, crashing into his arms and wrapping him in a hug as he lets out a soft grunt in surprise. "I'm late," I say into his neck. "I overslept and I turned my volume off because this town never has breaking news and—"

"You came." His arms tighten around me.

I want to stay just like this, wrapped in his strong embrace, my face buried against him, breathing him in. But the disbelief and wonder in his voice makes me straighten and meet his beautiful caramel eyes. They're soft and full of love, and the magnitude of everything that's happened in the past fifteen minutes finally crashes into me.

This man.

This man.

This wonderful, ridiculous, kind-hearted, pseudo-cowboy man. "I love you, too," I say, my voice cracking. "Of course I love you."

The smile that blooms across his face is bright enough to rival the sun. "You do?"

God, my heart. "I do." We hug again. I never want to go this long without the feel of his body against my own again.

He pulls away, taking my hand and guiding us to a nearby bench. "I have more to say."

"It doesn't matter." I face him on the bench, tucking one leg up and reaching for his hands.

"It does to me." He takes a deep breath, his gaze running the length of my body and back again. Amusement flickers in his eyes. "You really *did* just roll out of bed, didn't you?"

I swat at him. "I told you. Agatha was banging on my window like a crazy woman."

"I'm glad she did."

God, I missed his voice. I missed *him.* "Me, too."

He blows out another breath. "I'm so sorry. I'm sorry for hurting you, and I'm sorry for being an oblivious asshole. I was scared, Goldie. Scared that you'd get tired of me and realize you could have a life full of excitement and adventure without me weighing you down. Hell, I still am, but I'm working on that. You were"—he swallows— "too good to be true. You still are. I mean, there was no way it should have been as easy as it was with us. Who grows up together and then finds each other on a blind date app?" He laughs sadly.

"But we did," I whisper.

He looks at me with such tenderness. "We did. And all I could think about at first was how mad Willa would be, and of course, she gave me about ten tons of crap when she found out—"

"Yeah." I smile wryly. "She was surprised for about ten seconds, then wanted to know everything."

He chuckles. "Sounds like our Willa."

"She also made sure to tell me she didn't want to hear any juicy details about us in the bedroom."

He leans forward and cups my face, bringing us inches apart beneath the brim of his hat. "I missed you so much." When his lips meet mine, firm and soft all at once, it's like coming home.

I sigh into the kiss, melting against him like I always do, and whining a little when he pulls away a minute later.

Laughing, he leans back and tucks a strand of hair behind my ear. "We're in public, Golden."

Golden.

"Tell me more," I urge.

"More?"

"Don't you have more groveling to do?"

He snaps his fingers. "Right. I do." He shifts on the bench and meets my gaze once more. "I was a complete and total idiot. I didn't see what was right in my face, which was *you,* ready to love me for me, ready to give us a shot. I couldn't imagine being that lucky."

"Well, we *live* in Lucky," I grin. "Why wouldn't we be?"

"Tell me you forgive me," he says. "Because I love you so much. You're the only girl for me. I was an idiot never to see it all these years, a blind idiot not to realize it was you at the ball, and the biggest idiot to turn my back on you the second someone questioned whether this was real."

"About that—"

He puts a finger to my lips with a tender smile. "Let me finish. Ox and Reid weren't out to make me feel bad, and they weren't trying to make me second-guess anything. I'm the one who fell apart at the tiniest bit of questioning, and that's on me. Reid asked if this was serious, and I couldn't answer him. But being without you for even a few days showed me just how precious you are. How much you mean to me. How you've infiltrated every single part of my life, and how much I love having you in it. Without you, my days are dull and dark. You are my sunshine. I don't ever want to be without you again. Will you forgive me?"

I swallow back the lump in my throat and nod. "Of course I do."

He stands up and pulls me to him. "I love you." He lifts me off the ground and swings me around, whoops and cheers sounding in the distance.

"Do we have an audience?"

"Do you think Ox and Reid would have it any other way?" he counters, winking beneath the brim of his hat.

"Good point." I look up at him, reveling in his adoring smile. "Take me home, cowboy."

CHAPTER 38

GOLDIE

MATTY'S LIPS CRASH into mine the second we're in his house, his hands pulling me to him roughly. I go willingly, melting against him like always and eager to see more of what that thirst-trap video promised.

One button is undone on Matty's shirt before Kitty and Killer make themselves known, the big dog's head nudging against my leg while Killer yips excitedly at our feet.

"Fucking dogs," Matty mutters against my mouth.

I laugh. "Says the soft-hearted veterinarian."

Groaning, he pulls away and looks at them. "Outside."

But outside isn't what they want. They circle me, a tangle of legs and lolling tongues as I pet them and coo at them about the days I've not seen them. Matty pulls his boots off and hangs his hat, then leans against the door with his arms folded and a look of adoration on his face.

I raise my eyebrows. "See? You're a softie."

"Only for you." He pauses, then smirks. "And not in certain places."

Heat streaks through me at the way his eyes darken, and I leave the dogs where they are to make my way to him.

"There's my girl," he murmurs, pulling me flush against his body and slanting his mouth over mine.

Together, we move to his bedroom, where he presses me to the bedroom door and sinks to his knees. He looks up, his hands on my calves. "I wasn't sure I'd ever have you in my arms again."

My heart squeezes. I run my fingers through his hair and he closes his eyes, resting his forehead against my stomach. "I think we were inevitable, Matty."

He takes my shoes off. "Those days without you were torture. You've infiltrated me body and soul, Goldie. I don't ever want to be without you again."

"I'm yours." Then I leer at him. "Especially if you can promise me more of those videos."

He blushes. "Reid could moonlight as a photographer and videographer, I'm telling you."

"It was Reid?"

"Of course it was."

"Of course it was," I repeat, amused.

Matty tugs my skirt down, then laughs. "Are you wearing pajama bottoms under your skirt?"

"I flew out of my house to get to you, Matty. I barely brushed my teeth."

Growling appreciatively, he pulls the pajama bottoms off and brings his mouth to me, licking slowly up my center.

I gasp, immediately wanting more. But when I try to move us to the bed, Matty holds me in place, spreading me and licking deep, his eyes meeting mine as his lips close around my clit and he sucks.

My knees weaken as he continues, his tongue working wonders on my pussy like always, and my body heats, rushing to the brink faster than ever. "Matthew," I gasp.

He pushes two fingers inside me in answer, curling them as his mouth, his unbelievable mouth, continues to work me over. His fingers thrust, his tongue swirls, and waves of pleasure wrench their way through me as my hips buck. He takes me through the orgasm, humming against my clit, and when I finally take a breath, he eases back and stands up.

My chest heaves as I exhale. "HolycrapImissedthat."

He smirks. "*I* might have missed it more." Then he pulls the rest of my clothes off and I peel his off, too.

He spins us, walking me back and shoving me lightly onto the bed. "Tell me something, Miss Dash." He climbs on, his hair flopping into his eyes.

I raise an eyebrow. "Yes, Mr. Brodigan?"

He stops and wags a finger. "Ah-ah, that's *Doctor* Brodigan to you."

I smile. "Yes, *Doctor* Brodigan?"

"How would you liked to be fucked?"

I smile so broadly that I swear I sprain my cheek muscles. If that's even possible. "Deep and hard, Doctor."

He bends his head down to bite the inside of my thigh, hard enough that I hiss and my leg jerks in surprise. He holds my knee with one palm and looks up, his dark brown eyes hooded. "If you want it deep and hard, Miss Dash, then you need to listen to me."

I still, my body buzzing with anticipation. "Yes?"

"I want to watch you fuck yourself."

Heat floods my core as I rise onto my elbows. "Please tell me that means you're going to get yourself off at the same time."

His grin is filthy, and he nods slowly as he bites the inside of my other thigh, then swirls his tongue to soothe the mark he leaves behind.

I raise a hand.

"Yes?"

"Will you grab your hat?"

He chuckles darkly. "You and that damn hat." He licks up my thigh, then places a kiss right above my clit. "Do. Not. Move."

Not only do I not move, I barely freaking breathe while he's gone.

He's back in less than thirty seconds, striding through the bedroom door naked with only the black cowboy hat on.

"God, I love you. How the hell could you think *this* was boring?" I wave my hand in his direction.

He tips his hat. "We've already established that I'm a fool."

I hum in agreement.

He kneels at the end of the bed. "Now, lean against the headboard, my love. Knees spread. Show me that delicious pussy."

Warmth suffuses me as I get into position and do as he asks. "Your turn."

With a devilish grin, he takes his dick in his hand and slowly pumps, his abs and muscular thighs tensing.

Bringing my middle and ring fingers to my mouth, I suck them, then let go with a pop. "Matthew Brodigan, that thick dick is going to be my undoing." I trail my wet fingers lightly down my body, then push them into my pussy.

"Fuck, yes," he mutters, his gaze trained on my hand.

I match his rhythm, speeding up as he does. When I bring my other hand to my breast and squeeze it, pinching my nipple and arching my back, he shudders.

"Play with your clit," he orders, swirling his precum around and down his dick. He grips himself harder, pumping faster.

I match his speed again, only this time it's on my clit, and I feel myself getting close. "Matty."

"Just like that, Goldie." He curses again. "I'm—"

He starts to come, and I watch greedily, the vision of ecstasy on his face tipping me into my own orgasm.

I cry out, and his eyes snap to mine as we come together. Everything is in his expression: love, lust, wonder, adoration, *forever.* It's almost too much, but also, it's exactly perfect. Emotion rips through me, and I'm up and closing the distance to him before I take another breath, pulling his body to mine, kissing him as though he is the air I need to breathe.

Because he is. His arms wrap tight around me as we kneel on

the bed, our bodies pressed to each other, the hat knocked off in the process.

"Matthew," I gasp, "I need you. All of you. Please."

"You gotta give me a minute, baby." He laughs softly against my lips.

I grind against him. "I'm aching, Matthew. Please," I repeat.

"Fuck, Goldie," he growls. "What am I going to do with you?"

"Hard and deep," I say, sucking the skin on his neck. "Hard and so fucking deep."

He curses again, shoving a hand between us and grabbing me between the legs, his palm pressed against my clit and two thick fingers pushing into me.

"Yes," I hiss. "More." He goes harder, understanding what I need implicitly. But I'm out of my mind with it. All this love, all this emotion, it's so much and it feels like I'm crawling out of my skin. "I need you to come inside me."

"Babe," he breathes. "Are you sure?"

I yank the back of his hair, *hard*. "Matty," I growl. "I swear to God—"

He gets it. The next second, he throws me to the mattress and spreads my legs, thrusting into me so hard my head slams into the wooden headboard.

"Fuck *yes!*" I yell.

He grunts in response, burying himself to the hilt as my head hits the headboard and the headboard smacks the wall. It's fucking *everything*. And I need it again.

He cradles my head for the third and fourth and however many times he slams into me. This is possession. This is instinct. And as he fucks me, I understand that this, right here, is what I've craved. What *he's* craved. We've both needed it, this animalistic coming together. It strips everything away and leaves only us, our eyes never leaving each other's as he pounds into me.

But I need more. We shift, and I get on my knees as he kneels behind me. He bends down to lick my center, groaning as I push back onto his face. I want him covered in me.

He rises and positions himself behind me. "On your elbows."

I lower, and am immediately rewarded with his dick. His thick dick, going so fucking deep that it nearly hurts.

It's perfect.

It's even better when he brings a hand around to my clit and swirls a finger around it. "Up."

I lift, pressing my back to his front, and he keeps pumping into me. Turning my head, I pull his lips to mine. "I love you so fucking much," I gasp out, breathless.

"I love you, too, Golden."

And that's exactly what I need. I grip the back of his hair as he holds me in place, his fingers on my clit as he pushes into me over and over. His dick throbs as he groans my name against my neck, spilling inside me, and I fucking love it. When my own orgasm comes a moment later, it's luxurious and full, a sunrise of pleasure, wrenching through me as my body shudders with release.

We breathe, still holding tight to each other. Matty kisses my neck, and I gradually let go of his hair as his hands stroke over me, down my arms and up my stomach.

"Can we do that every day?" I murmur against his lips when he leans down for another kiss.

"Absolutely."

"Then you're forgiven."

He grins. "I thought you'd already forgiven me."

I shift so we're facing each other, still on our knees, the bed covers strewn around us. "Say it again."

His eyes sparkle. "I love you. With all that I am, and all that I ever will be, I love you."

My heart bursts.

CHAPTER 39

EPILOGUE

"ARE YOU SURE?" Agatha looks at the key, then shifts a worried glance between me and Goldie.

Goldie laughs. "Agatha, I'm sure. Besides, isn't it time for another *lucky* resident to move in and find the love of their life? I hear Darcy's getting tired of living above the hardware store."

"Well, I *am* two for two." She sniffs.

I bite my lip. She is no such thing, but we'll never tell her.

"And we're just as happy as Willa and Reid," Goldie assures her.

"But you've only been dating for…" She trails off, then furrows her brow. "How long *have* you two been dating?"

I pull Goldie to me and kiss her temple. "Five months."

"Six, if you count when we first connected on the app," Goldie corrects.

"Whatever you say." Winking, I jerk my thumb over my shoulder. "I'm going to grab more boxes."

"Spoken like a man who's learned all the right lessons." Agatha is as satisfied as a cat in the sun.

Goldie giggles and begins moving backward. "We'll be out of

your hair in just a few more minutes. I've already cleaned it top to bottom—and I hand-washed the doilies."

"I'll leave it empty just in case you change your mind!" Agatha calls. "At least for a month!"

In the kitchen, I pull Goldie to me for one last kiss in the cottage that's been her home for the past year. "You hand-washed her doilies?" I ask incredulously.

"Of *course* I did. Those things are legendary."

"They're something, all right."

"Come on, cowboy. Let's get these last boxes loaded."

We meet Willa and Reid for Mexican later that night to celebrate Goldie moving in with me. I can't help but remember the last time all of us were here. I'd turned thirty and was the loneliest I'd ever been. But now? I've made some major headway, including calling my parents and inviting them for a visit. I don't know that they'll ever think I'm exciting, exactly, but given that we haven't seen each other in a couple years, them coming home for a visit is a good start.

I shift in my seat, patting my pocket to make sure the box is still there. Reid, ever the observer, raises an eyebrow as he takes a sip of beer. I shake my head slightly, not quite ready to do it, but also not *not* quite ready.

Basically, I am a nervous mess and can't handle anything right now.

Also, I do *not* plan on proposing to the love of my life in Los Amigos, no matter that it's our favorite restaurant in town.

Carmen comes over with a round of tequila. We pass it around, and Willa starts the toast.

"To family."

Goldie is next. "To new beginnings."

"To love," I offer.

"To my future wife," Reid finishes.

We'd all been moving our glasses to our lips, but at Reid's words, we stop and stare.

"What did you just say?" Willa says.

And that mother fucker goes down on his knee and takes Willa's hand in his.

"Eep!" Goldie's hands fly to her mouth.

Willa stares at Reid.

And right when I'm trying to decide if I'm pissed that he's stealing my thunder—okay, potential thunder, whatever—I see Ox appear out of nowhere, his phone trained on Reid and Willa and out of Willa's line of sight.

God damn, Reid's good.

Reid takes a deep breath and lets it out, smiling with absolute love at my best friend. "Willa Dean Dash."

"Reid," she whispers shakily.

He gives a soft laugh as he reaches up to wipe her cheek with his thumb. "Don't cry yet, sweetheart. Let me get the words out."

She sniffs and nods.

"From the very beginning, I was absolutely smitten with you. You walked up to the table, dropped your pen, banged your head, and swept me off my feet. And even though you spent way too much time running away from me, I knew all I had to do was keep wearing those running shorts and I'd wear you down."

Willa snorts out a laugh, and I can see how red her cheeks are burning.

"Ah, you laugh, but it worked." He winks at her, then reaches into his shirt pocket and pulls out a ring. "Willa, will you do me the honor of being my wife?"

"Has that ring been in there the whole time?" Willa asks.

Goldie huffs. "Answer the man!"

"Yes!" Willa says. "Yes, yes, yes."

Reid slides the ring onto her finger, then stands and pulls her to him. The entire restaurant explodes into applause, and the Mariachi band appears and begins to play. Carmen and others pop streamers over the couple, and in moments it's clear we are in the middle of one heck of a celebration.

Goldie leans into me. "Did you know about this?"

If you only knew. "I didn't," I tell her, "but this is amazing."

I give Reid a congratulatory handshake that he turns into a hug while Goldie squeals and grabs Willa into a fierce embrace. Ox ambles up, waving his cell phone.

"Did you get it?" Reid asks.

"Of course I did," Ox answers. "It's already sent."

Finally, Goldie releases Willa, and I get to congratulate my best friend. Pulling her into a hug, I squeeze tight. "I'm so happy for you. You deserve all the happiness in the world."

She sniffs. "So do you." We break apart, and she wipes at her eyes, smiling wider than I've ever seen. "Why do I keep crying? Holy shit, Matty, I'm getting *married!*"

I hug her again. "Yeah you are!"

It's another hour before Goldie and I get home. We let the dogs out, and while Goldie's back is turned, I slip the box out and hide it. Tonight was for Willa and Reid, but it won't be long before I propose to my golden girl.

I pull her to me in the dark bedroom, her soft skin and plush lips a heaven that I'm still not sure I deserve, but that I'll do whatever it takes to be worthy of. I'll do anything for this woman. When she tells me she loves me, I whisper it back, then I show her. Again, and again. Forever, and always.

Also by Valerie Pepper

Guided to Love

The Mechanic's Guide to Getting the Boss's Daughter (series prequel novella)

The Widow's Guide to Second Chances (Book 1)

The Barista's Guide to The Perfect Steam (Book 2)

The Grump's Guide to Chaos (Book 3)

Sacred River

Love Potion No. 69 (Novella, Book 1)

Karaoke Chemistry (Book 2)

Lucky in Love

Dining for Love (Book 1)

Dashing for Love (Book 2)

Standalone Novellas

Naughty All The Way (November 2023)

To Have and To Scold in the *Holidays & Hook-Ups* anthology by The New Romance Cafe (June 2023 - limited edition)

ABOUT THE AUTHOR

Valerie Pepper is an incurable optimist and a firm believer in the girl getting the guy, or the guy getting the girl, or the girl getting the girl, or the guy getting the guy, or basically any way it needs to happen to make a real-life happily ever after, even if it takes more than one try.

When she's not writing, you can find her reading, walking, listening to whatever music suits her mood, and hanging out with her family. She's fascinated with the idea of a capsule wardrobe, but loves clothes and shoes and boots far too much to make a real go of it.

She's currently living out her own happily ever after in Birmingham, Alabama, with her family and maaaaaybe too many shoes. Learn more at www.authorvaleriepepper.com.